A FAIRY AWESOME STORY

Aiden

COPYRIGHT

Copyright © 2020 by Ellie Aiden

Cover Art by Ellie Aiden

All rights reserved. Except as permitted by the U.S. Copyright Act of 1976, no part of this publication may be reproduced, distributed, or transmitted in any form or by any means without the prior written permission of the author.

First Edition: June 2020

The characters and events portrayed in this book are strictly fictitious. Any similarities to locations, characters, events, or persons, living or dead, is purely coincidental.

TABLE OF CONTENTS

Bestie From Another Teste
Hottie McHotterson
Roller-Coaster Ride
Stage Five Clinger
Thirsty Bitch
Rule Breaking
Freaking Leprechaun
Bee Stings
Ninja-Spy-Snoop-Fest
The Moment We've All Been Waiting For
Mother Flipping Leprechauns
Spidey Senses
Ransom Video
The Succubus Of The Fairy World
Ex-Nay On The Magi-Cay
No Choice
Epilogue—

BESTIE FROM ANOTHER TESTE

"I said, go to your room, young fairy."

"O. M. Gee. Dad, I'm a freaking adult. I'm nineteen years old. You can't make me go to my room." I throw my hands in the air, making sure he sees when I roll my eyes not once but twice.

His arm flies out, his finger pointing to the stairs. "When you start acting like an adult, I'll treat you like one. Now go!" His voice echoes through the large open space.

"Ugh."

I'm tired of arguing, so I stomp past him, making sure I make as much noise on the way up as possible. At the top of the stairs, I practically drag my feet as I make my way through the long corridor to my room. It's the last one on the right, and after I step through the threshold I slam the door to make myself feel better. It doesn't.

Crossing to my bed, I turn, giving it my back before falling backwards and landing with a small bounce. I grab the edge of my white down comforter, pulling it as I roll so I'm wrapped up like a burrito. Snuggling in, I close my eyes, trying and failing to tamp down on my anger at the way my dad treats me. He didn't used to be like this. Well, that's not entirely true. He's always been the overbearing parent, but it's been worse in the last year. Our whole relationship has changed. As far as fairies go, I'm basically an adult, so I really thought he would've backed off by now. No such luck.

I know what the problem is, though, and it isn't my age.

It's the fact that I'm the heir to the f'ing Seelie throne. It's not like I asked for this shit. It's not my fault my dad wasn't gifted with the mark of the Seelie by God. It's also not my fault that my mom was killed last year in an Unseelie raid or that my little sister is only six. But even though none of those things are my fault, I'm damn sure gonna pay for them.

My whole life changed when my mom was killed last year. As devastated as I was, hell, still am, her life ending forever changed the course of mine. Only a Seelie-marked fairy can sit on the throne, and while my dad doesn't have the mark, my mom did. Which means I would've had decades possibly before I had to ascend if she hadn't been killed. But now, my uncle Rowan, or, excuse me, King Rowan sits on the throne and he announced last month he intends to step down in one year's time. That means that I have eleven months left before my whole life is ruined. Okay, yes, I realize I'm being dramatic, but damn. How is it fair that someone else gets to dictate my life?

Fair or not, part of me doesn't want the throne while the other part does, and I've sort of been rebelling ever since he made the announcement. One such act of rebellion is what led me to being grounded to my room at nineteen years old. Okay, yes, my bestie and I did get drunk on fairy wine and steal the Leprechaun ambassador's watch. We were going to give it back. We were. It was just a joke. I just wanted to have a little fun. Why can't my dad see that? This is my last hoorah before I suddenly have to behave as if I have a stick up my ass for the rest of my life. Too soon it'll be all crowns and big gowns, full hair and makeup, and plastering on a fake smile for all of Fay to see. I don't wanna. Ugh.

I throw the comforter back, flailing my arms like a toddler and decide a hot bath is exactly what I need. I stomp across the room even though no one can see me, and slip into my ensuite. With a snap of my fingers the chandelier above me springs to life, lighting the room as I cross to the porcelain claw-foot tub. I get the water running at just the right temperature, a.k.a. scalding hot, and step back to strip. Throwing my clothes in a pile in the middle of the floor, I stick a pinky toe in to test that it's perfect, and seeing that it is, I practically roll in. My skin immediately turns an alarming shade of pink, but I don't care. This water is about to wash all my cares away.

I pour in a dollop of the calming bubble bath my dad got me last year for my birthday, and watch as it swirls, mixing with the water. It starts to foam, the pink bubbles covering my entire body, and I breath in the relaxing aroma of lavender.

Lying my head back on my feather soft bath pillow, I try to let myself fall asleep, but after several minutes it's clear this isn't working. I blame my dad for this. He and the stupid throne are causing me serious anxiety. I'll be on anti-anxiety meds by the time I'm twenty if something doesn't give. And this stupid mark. I'm starting to wish I didn't even have this damn thing.

I roll my wrist over, resting it lightly on the edge of the tub, the cool porcelain feeling good against my fevered skin. I run my finger around the edge, the shape in the form of two wings. Fairy wings. I've always thought that was stupid. Not all fairies even have wings. *I* don't have wings, so why God chose this design is beyond me. Why he chose to gift the mark to me is also a wonder. I'm not special, not in the grand scheme of things anyway. I mean yes, because of the mark I can do things other fairies can't. My magic is stronger. *I'm* stronger. But without it, I'm just a normal, old fairy.

I blow a breath out through my teeth and wonder how he chooses. There are so many types of fairies, and in each type there are numerous subcategories. Any fairy can be Seelie. If they're gifted the mark, that is. The mark appears within two weeks after birth, and there's no way to get it off. Trust me, I've tried. If the mark doesn't appear at two weeks, you wait another two weeks to see if the fairy will be marked by the Devil as UnSeelie. If not, then you're just your average, run-of-the-mill fairy. God, I wish I was just a normal fairy. Well, that's not entirely true. I like the perks. I want the mark gone, but I want to keep the perks. Is that too much to ask for? I like to be waited on hand and foot. That does *not* make me entitled. Okay, it does a little, but whatever.

I snatch a washcloth from the shelf and scrub my body, taking extra time on my wrist, praying this will be the time the damn thing comes off. When I see it won't, I settle for a quick glamour, and I watch as the outline fades to nothing but clear, pale skin. I do that a lot and it drives my dad crazy. He always says one of these days I'm going to glamour that thing away in the wrong setting, and something bad is going to happen. Well it hasn't so far, and it symbolizes my oppression, so if I want to forget about it every once in a while, I don't see why it matters.

Sliding down, I submerge my whole body under the water's surface, strands of my lavender hair floating across my face. I open my eyes, relishing in the burn the bubbles cause. With a thought, I create a tiny cyclone next to me and watch as it spins wildly. It doesn't take long for me to get bored with that, and I let it die down, running my hands through my hair. I let loose one bubble of air at a time until there's nothing left in my lungs, and then, even though I don't have to, I come up for air. I wipe the water from my eyes and…My heart jumps into my throat. "Shit, what the hell, man?" There's nothing I hate worse than someone getting the drop on me.

I glare at Tab, my bestie from another teste, as she stands with a hand on each hip. Her iridescent-blue hair is pulled up in a messy top-knot, and her green eyes are filled with ire. I'm not sure what she has to be pissed about. I'm the one that's grounded, not her. I jerk my head at her in the universal sign for, *what's your problem*, while simultaneously reaching for my favorite purple towel.

"Even drunk I told you we were gonna get caught," she blabs, taking a step back to allow me to slip over the edge of the tub. "And now you're grounded. Is he even going to let you go to Tib's birthday party tomorrow night?" Her hands leave her hips as she crosses her arms against her chest.

"No clue." I shrug, drying myself off and pushing past her. "But honestly, Tib is an ass. I don't even wanna go."

She throws her hands in the air, stomping to the bed before plopping down. "So what, I'm just supposed to go by myself? Absolutely not."

I slip on my absolute favorite yoga pants, followed by an oversized tank before turning back to face her. "What do you want from me?"

She flops back, looking like a fish out of water as she flails her arms and legs. Every few seconds she peeks an eye open to make sure I'm watching her fit, and I roll my eyes before joining her on the bed. I lie back, turning my head so we're eye to eye.

Tab and I have been best friends since we were in diapers. She isn't a royal, but she is Seelie. Her dad works in the palace as a guard, which means while he was guarding me as a young fairy, Tab was always right there with me. We've gotten into a lot of trouble together over the years, and while she can be a bad influence, I wouldn't want to do life without her.

She scoots closer, using a perfect pouty lip on me. Her skin shimmers, her Selkie traits prominent. Her skin is looking a little dry, which means she probably hasn't wet her skin in a while. Unlike what some think, Selkies don't have to remain in the water, but if they're out for too long, it can do a lot of irreversible damage to their skin. Selkies aren't common in the capital, mostly because of a lack of salt water sources. While it isn't a requirement, they do prefer it, so most of them live near the Yellow Sea. I was always surprised that Tab's dad kept her here. Selkies are natural shapeshifters, but they can only shift in the presence of salt water, so keeping her here is like asking her to go against her very nature. I'm not complaining though. If she ever does leave, I'll drag her back, kicking and screaming.

Tab thumps me on the shoulder, drawing my attention back. "Ell, not wanting to go to a party sure doesn't seem like something a girl would do who has committed the next eleven months to absolute debauchery. I guess you're just not very good at this. Tib may be an ass, but his parties are filled with sex, drugs, and alcohol. You're like the worst Nymph ever. What kind of Nymph is still a virgin at nearly twenty years old?" She throws the question out there, knowing it's a low blow.

I gasp, pressing my hand to my chest in mock offense. "How dare you? I'm a virgin by choice, hooker."

"Oh my God, come on. We have less than one year to have all the sex before you're suddenly under house arrest." She lets out a dramatic sigh, peeking at me through the corner of one eye. "But I guess if you're not up to it…" She lets her last word trail off, waiting for me to take the bait like she knows I will.

I snatch the pillow above my head, smacking her in the face because I guess we're sneaking out to go to a party. I'm so going to get grounded for this. Well, I guess, *more* grounded.

***

I pull my mini–skirt down for the nine-billionth time as it rides up revealing my ass cheeks yet again. I don't mind showing a little bit of skin, but this black leather mini Tab let me borrow is ridiculous. Although, I do look hot, if I do say so myself. We paired the leather mini with a white sequin tube top and black four-inch, red-bottom heels. I decided to wear my hair down, even after Tab begged me to go with an up-do, and even though she was mad at me, she still did an awesome job on my smokey eye makeup, set off with a fire-engine red lipstick.

I glance at her out of the corner of my eye. She looks great too, and between the two of us, we probably won't even have to *try* to get laid. Honestly, my princess status alone should pull in enough P to last a lifetime. I roll my eyes at myself, knowing I talk a big game but never back it up. And despite that, as we make an entrance at Tib's birthday bash, our heads held high, everyone around stops to stare and we are really feeling ourselves with all the attention. I put an extra sway in my step as we move further down the side of the estate, and Tab notices, rolling her eyes with a giggle.

As we get close to the back, I hear the thumping of music and feel pissed that Tib is better at being a Nymph than I am. Tab was right, his parties really are the craziest. It's times like these I wish I could just do what I'm supposed to do. Don't get me wrong, I'll smoke weed all day. I have zero issues with getting drunk constantly. And I don't mind a good make-out session regardless of who's watching, but when it comes to actually doing the deed, something keeps holding me back. It feels like the universe doesn't want me to make that jump. I probably just need to ignore the universe, and I think tonight may be my night.

The loud bass from speakers coming up on our right vibrates my body as the raging party finally comes into view. Fairies are packed on an impromptu dance floor set up in front of a small stage where D.J. Sprite stands swaying to the beat. She hovers above the stage, her bright-pink hair spiked to the heavens as she holds her purple head phones to her ear.

The skunky scent of weed wafts toward me from a group of Brownies on my right, while a mix of Merpeople, Kelpies, and a Dryad play beer pong on my left. I spot the Elves right off the bat. A group of eight, each of them with a goblet of fairy wine in hand, stand off to the side, their noses in the air as they look down on everyone. Gawd, I hate Elves. Such snobs. Seriously, they all walk around with their noses in the air, thinking they're better than everyone else. Not to mention, Elves are the most likely fairy to be gifted with the mark of the Devil.

I nearly trip as Tab grabs my hand, yanking me through the crowd toward the bar. The long wooden surface is surrounded by dozens of people waiting for drinks, but that won't be a problem for us. Remember when I said perks?

I squeeze my way in-between two Nymphs, and with a quick wave of my hand, the bartender stops everything he's doing to take my order. Yeah, this is the part I like about being a royal. Wait on me hand and foot, peasants. JK.

"Two, no, make that four fairy wines, please."

He turns, zipping left and right, grabbing goblets and wine as he goes. "Coming right up, Your Highness."

Ahh, that's what I like to hear.

Within seconds our drinks are slid across the bar, and grabbing one in each hand, we move away from the crowd and find a spot to people watch while we get a couple drinks in our system. We clink our goblets together and practically down the first one in one go, chunking the empty container on a nearby table before moving on to the next. I'm halfway through my second drink when a hot-as-sin Elf passes by, and Tab bumps me with her shoulder.

"Okay, I know we hate Elves, but *damn*," Tab drags out the last word, pumping her brows up and down.

"Yeah, I could get down with that."

She gives me a doubtful look as she says, "Oh really? Well then, Princess, by all means, go get you a piece."

Shit, I should've seen that coming. "Well I mean, he's an Elf, so he's definitely an ass, and I'm really just not in the mood for 'tude."

"Uh-huh."

I ignore her, opting instead to down the last of my wine before traipsing past her to order another. We spend the next two hours putting a dangerous amount of alcohol in our systems, while watching everyone else make asses of themselves. My head swims and my nose is numb, a sign I'm nearly to my limit. I place my empty goblet on the table, turning to Tab to see if she's ready to leave.

"Maybe we should go. I'm way…to drunk for this…shit." I stumble on the words as she takes two long swigs of her wine.

Setting her goblet down, we turn to leave but are stopped by a group of palace guards, although from the looks of them, they're off duty. Unfortunately, Nyx is with them, and while we've been friends for years, I can't guarantee he'll risk his job by not telling my dad that I snuck out.

"I'm pretty sure I heard you were grounded and not to leave the palace," Nyx says, one hand shoved casually in his pocket as two other guards flank him.

"We were just leaving," I assure him. "There's no reason for you to tell my dad, right?"

His lips purse as he raises a brow. "I don't know, what's in it for me?"

"Friends with benefits," Tab blurts, dead serious.

My jaw drops, forming an O, and I can't believe this little

wench just said that. I'm so going to murder her later. Bitch is trying to get cut.

Nyx was taking a drink and with her words, he snorts, the drink spewing back out. He looks to Tab and then me as his friends die laughing. Tab is close enough to me that I'm able to reach between us and give her a little pinch, forcing her to let out a yelp.

"What?" She squeaks, clueless. "You said you wanted to get laid tonight."

Oh my god, you are so dead, Tabitha Rain.

Nyx's eyes grow wider, if that's possible, and I'm completely mortified. I don't know the other two guards with him, but they're both keeled over laughing. I may never live this moment down.

The guard with jet black hair slicked away from his forehead let's out a snort as he tries to catch his breath. "Is that so, Princess? Well, I can help you with that. In fact, all three of us would be happy to help you out. I bet Nyx would like to do some very naughty things…"

Nyx turns to him, and I swear I hear him growl as he gives him a warning look. Turning back to me, his features change to a look of what I would call pity. "We most certainly will *not* be helping her out with that."

I know hurt flashes in my eyes, and I don't even know why. It's not like I want to fuck Nyx, but damn, that was a little harsh. I'm fuckable, right?

Nyx takes a step in my direction, effectively cutting off his friends. "You need to go home right now, Princess."

Who the hell is he to tell *me* what to do? So what if he's a freaking guard. I'm the fucking princess of all Seelie, and he should *damn* well remember that. "How dare you? What gives you the right to tell me what to do?"

He takes another step in my space, leaning forward and his next words are meant only for me. "Please, Ell. I don't want to have to tell your dad. But everyone has seen you tonight, including these two assholes. I'll try to keep them from talking, but I need you to go home, please." His cheek brushes against mine as he pulls away, a plea swirling in his lavender eyes.

"Ugh," I sigh. "Fine." And turning to Tab, I add, "Let's go. This party is lame anyways."

I grab her arm, dragging her drunk ass away as the two guards with Nyx continue to make fun of us. Fuck them. I'll get them back later. In case you didn't know, fairies are known for being tricksters, and I am the absolute best.

We make it out front and I check the time. I giggle, seeing that it's 2:00 a.m. I don't know why that's so funny, but it is. I'm so screwed. There's no way we don't get caught, but I guess we're about to try.

We stumble through the streets of the capital, and I'm kicking myself for how tonight went. I really am the worst Nymph. I spent hours drunk at a party filled with hot fairies, and not only did I mostly keep to myself, but I'm no closer to losing my v-card. Most fairies are naturally promiscuous, but Nymphs even more so. How do you think they came up with the term nymphomaniac? Even Tab has a random thing happening with one of the palace guards, while I'm over here practically a prude. Sure I've made out with more fairies than I can count, but anything beyond that, well, I haven't even come close. I've had a few boyfriends here and there, but I never had the desire to make the jump. Actually, that's not entirely true. I have more than enough desire. I blame this on the choice of fairies. Sure they're all hot, well, most of them, but they're also a-holes. I just can't get past that. Tab says it shouldn't have anything to do with that; that I need to test out the goods so I can decide what I like, but that mentality hasn't worked out for me so far. Yes, I want someone to bend me over and fuck the shit out of me, but I also want them to buy me dinner first. Is that too much to ask for?

And then there's the whole thing with Nyx. I hate that his words bothered me, and maybe that isn't how he meant it, but it damn sure seemed like he meant he didn't want me. I'm probably having unreasonable drunk emotions. I guess I'll see how I feel about it tomorrow. No, you know what? I won't see how I feel about it tomorrow. Fuck Nyx.

Tab trips in front of me, pulling me from my thoughts as she face-plants. I can't help the laugh that bursts free from my lips, and it grows even louder when she begins uncontrollably giggling. I shush her, bending down to help her up, but I'm clearly too drunk for all that. I topple forward, landing on top of her, an '*oomph*' forced from my gut. I know we need to be quiet or risk being caught, but I can't seem to stop laughing and neither can Tab.

I don't know how long we lie there drunk-laughing, but just as we start to get it together, an orb of light appears above us, lighting our surroundings, and my dad's pissed off face comes into view.

Well, shit.

HOTTIE MCHOTTERSON

To say I was in deep shit last night is a total understatement. In fact, I don't think I've ever seen my dad so mad. He was screaming so loud after he drug Tab and I both into the throne room, my uncle heard him from his private wing and came down to try to calm him. For every bit the straight-laced fairy my dad is, my uncle is the opposite. Sure he knows how and when to be serious, but he tends to be pretty laid back. The stories I've heard about the parties he used to throw would make you blush. Hell, they make *me* blush. My mom told me about this one orgy...no, I'm just going to leave that to the imagination.

Anyway, after two hours of my dad reading us the riot-act, he'd sent Tab home in the care of a guard, and he'd practically drug me to my room before locking the door. That's right, I am officially locked in my room. I mean yes, technically, I can get out if I want, but still. This is ridiculous. I'm an adult and he does nothing but treat me like a child. I know he loves me, but I just wish he showed it more often instead of constantly being so harsh and overbearing.

Last night, though, I hadn't really cared about him locking me in my room. All I'd been thinking about was getting a quick snack and then passing out, but now, I'm pissed. I can't live under these conditions another second. I need to get out of this palace, and I *need* to live a little. I need to have the opportunity to try all the things, to make mistakes before I'm tied down to the throne for the rest of my life. But I know as long as I'm in Fay, my dad will find me and drag me back, kicking and screaming. I could go to Earth, but it's forbidden. Seelie fairies are the most powerful of all the fairies, and because fairy magic is so directly tied to Earth's energy, weird and sometimes bad shit happens when we go there. A regular 'ole fairy can go, play their tricks, and come back without any real issues, but if a Seelie goes, well, let's just say that's how both world wars happened. I'd really hate to cause a war all for the sake of a little fun, but I'm running out of options here.

The Office plays quietly on my Earth Vision as I scrub my hands down my face, trying to talk myself out of the decision I know I've already made. Maybe it won't be so bad. I'll just go, have a little fun for a few weeks, and slip right back to Fay. No big deal. It'll be fine. Or it won't, and my fun little visit could turn into a zombie apocalypse. You know, whatever.

I plop down on my setae just as Jim proposes to Pam. Aww, this is one of my favorite episodes. Thank God for Earth Vision. The entertainment choices in Fay might as well be from the dark ages. Fairies still think the opera and ballets are the highest form of entertainment, and while I have seen a few that are worth the watch, there is nothing that compares to *The Office*.

With a snap of my fingers, the screen on my wall turns black, ending my temporary distraction. Pacing a circle around my room, I weigh all the pros and cons. I don't know why though. I know deep down I've already made the decision.

I suck in a deep breath as I admit it to myself. I'm going. The only question now is whether or not I should tell Tab? She's gonna be so pissed if I leave without telling her. Hell, she's gonna be pissed if I don't invite her. But every person I tell, and the more fairies that go, the more likely some bad shit will happen. It'll be too much energy and it'll lead my dad to me much quicker than if I go alone. No, I'm just going to go and beg for forgiveness later.

I climb to my feet, rushing to my closet to grab a bag before I change my mind. Chunking a few of my favorite outfits inside, I start cramming shoes in next. I'm out of room within seconds, and realize I'm going to need a second bag.

Eight pairs of shoes, my entire makeup caboodle, and my

favorite little-black dress later, I've got two bags draped over my shoulder. I storm to the door, determination set on my features as I muster up a little magic. I focus on the locked door, and I wonder why in Fay my dad would think he could use a regular lock to keep me in. I know it's not that he trusts me. That ship has sailed.

My magic manifests in the form of a purple mist. It seeps from my fingers to the knob, and hearing a click, I slip out quietly. The hall is dark even though it's the middle of the day, and I sneak through the halls like a total ninja. I really should've worn black. It would have gone well with this whole sneaking thing I have going on.

It takes me a good ten minutes to make it to the staff entrance, and with a quick glance around to be sure the coast is clear, I quietly slip out and make a bee-line for the south wall. I'm embarrassed to say how long it takes me to get over said wall, so I won't. But once I'm on the other side, I head for the nearest portal. It's only about an hour walk, but five minutes in I'm really wishing I'd worn different shoes. These damn heels were a mistake. But I didn't have any more room in my bag and I really wanted to bring these. It would've been nice if I could have used one of the portals inside the palace, but unfortunately, I would've been caught the second I powered it up. Those things are like a freaking beacon.

The big ash tree comes into view and I know I'm close. When I see the widow's hut, I slow before ducking down behind a large fir tree. The widow may be an outcast, but she wouldn't think twice about turning me in to my dad, if for no other reason than she would expect a reward.

Smoke billows from her chimney, and given the current temperature, I'd say she isn't heating her house. That means she's either brewing a potion or lunch, which means she'll be distracted and I can slip right through. I pull out my brown leather pouch from its place attached to my jeans, and slipping two fingers inside, I pull out the tiniest amount of fairy dust. Being a Seelie royal, I'm one of the strongest fairies in the realm, so I don't need dust for everything I do, but portals require a special sort of magic and it can't be powered up without a little bit of dust.

Slipping out from behind my hiding place, I'm careful where I step as I eat up the last few feet of distance before chunking the dust over the thin, black split between the realms. The portal springs to life, the tear growing bigger and bigger as it lets off an immense amount of blue light. I shield my eyes as I stumble back a step.

Crap, why does it have to be so bright?

My head jerks toward the house, and seeing no movement, I let out a sigh of relief before turning back to the now massive tear in the space between Earth and Fay. I grab a hold of a little magic, encasing myself with a quick glamour. I look fairly human, but I don't want to stand out where I'm going, wherever that is.

Where *do* I want to go? I really should've made this decision before now. I can't go somewhere obvious. The very first spot my dad would look for me would be New York or L.A. No, I need a small town.

I close my eyes, stepping one foot in the portal as I totally pull something random out of my ass.

Electra, Texas.

What? I heard my mom mention it once. Something about ley lines.

My stomach does a flip as I'm pulled through space. Everything within sight is black, with floating ribbons of rainbow colored light. I've done this before, so I'm used to the beauty of it. What I'm not used to is the vacuum of space. That's not something you ever get used to. On instinct I suck in a breath, and my lungs constrict. Just as I'm about to panic, I feel my feet hit solid ground. Squinting one eye open, *um*, I really should've thought this through. Maybe done a little research. This isn't just a small town, it's miniscule. Where the heck are all the people? From the looks of it, I'm in a downtown area, but there's not a soul in sight. Also, by downtown, I mean like three buildings, *maybe*. Okay yes, that's an exaggeration, but damn. What the hell do people do here? What am *I* going to do here? I wanted fun, and I can't imagine they have a lot of that here.

I spin in a circle, feeling very overwhelmed. No, scratch that, underwhelmed is a better word. Maybe I should just go home. If I leave right now, I can probably get back to my room before anyone notices I'm missing.

No, Ell. You're spiraling. You can do this.

The pep talk is not helping, but as I spin one more time, I see an elderly gentleman, cowboy hat and all, step out of the drug store across the street from me. I wonder what sort of drugs they sell as I step off the sidewalk and approach the man with my best smile. He's tall and slender with a small hunch in his back. His eyes are kind though, which gives me the confidence I need.

I clear my throat. "Sup?"

Maybe that wasn't the best greeting, because from the looks of it he thinks I'm a disrespectful little shit. Whatever though, I'm nervous. Cut me some slack.

"Ya must be lost," he remarks as he repositions the sack he's carrying. "You lookin' for somethin'?"

Well, that's quite a southern drawl ya got there, mister. Of course, I don't say that to him. I'm not a complete idiot.

"Um, yes. I am lost. Well, sort of. Actually, I mean to be here, I just don't know where to go now. See I need a place to live."

A look of compassion melts his features as he moves a little closer. I'm not uncomfortable yet, but he's got about another foot and then it's evasive maneuvers or magic. I hate to use magic on a little old man, but I will if I have to.

He repositions the sack again and I get the impression it might be heavy. "You're homeless? You a runaway, sweetie?"

"Uh, not really, but I guess. Um, can I help you to your car with that? It looks heavy."

My hand thrusts out and he doesn't hesitate handing it over. He nods his head toward a beat-up red pickup parked at the curb a few spaces down before turning and expecting me to follow. He's slow moving, but I don't mind. Where the hell else do I need to be? I honestly half expect a tumbleweed to roll across the street at any second. I wonder if when I stepped through that portal something went horribly wrong and I was thrown back in time. Back to the wild, wild west. Yeah, I know, I'm grasping.

As he opens the passenger door with a creak, he picks the conversation back up. "Not much 'round here, hun. There's a hotel out near edge of town, but I doubt you'd wanna stay there."

My hopes sink like a stone as I set the brown sack in his floorboard before stepping back out of the way. When the door slams, he turns back to face me, and I assume he'll be on his way. He passes me, moving around to the driver's side and stepping up on the side-step before opening the door. I give him the best smile I can muster, all things considered, and turn to leave.

"You said ya needed a job, right?"

His words stop me in my tracks, and I spin around with a flourish, a big smile on my face. "Yeah."

"Well, get in then. My wife and I'll put ya up, and a friend of mine is hiring out at The Oasis."

I squeal as I jump in the passenger side, not giving a single shit about stranger danger. If this old man is the killer, I'll cut off my left tit.

***

John, that's the old guy that most definitely is not the killer, had driven us back to his ranch down at least eight dirt roads. It really was a beautiful drive, and I'd enjoyed myself as we rode, the window down, my hair blowing in the breeze. When we pulled up in front of a cute, little white home, and his wife stepped out on the porch, I was blown away with how lucky I'd just gotten. Seriously, John and Midge are legit the definition of the grandparents everyone wants. Not that I would know because both sets of mine died before I was born, but they're what I imagine perfect grandparents to be. They even told me to call them Meemaw and Peepaw. Like I said, the cutest. My heart did a somersault.

Midge had been a little more inquisitive than John, but I got the distinct impression that John and Midge take in people all the time. Midge even made the comment that John had brought home another stray when she was on the phone after dinner. I didn't mind though because she'd followed that up with gushing about how beautiful I was, and even said something about setting me up with Sharon's son. Now, I don't know who Sharon is, but if her son is hot, I'm *so* in.

After she'd gotten off the phone, John had called his friend that apparently owns a tiny hole-in-the-wall bar, and was able to get me an audition as a waitress. I'd masked my power a little, just in case, and John drove me. He even said he'd be waiting outside to take me home when I got off. Home. He said home, y'all.

Eeek. I said y'all, y'all.

I know I was a little worried about this place, but so far everything is turning up roses for me in little, Electra, Texas.

And as I step through the threshold of The Oasis, I'm feeling even better about things. This is perfect. It's exactly what I wanted it to be. There are a few tables through the main area with a long bar on one side. The area around the bar is lit up with a bright-blue neon sign, giving off a somewhat seedy feeling, and I am so for it. The bar is lined with brown high-back stools on this side, and toward the back of the room, I can just make out a couple pool tables with neat little lights hanging overhead. There's only a handful of people here, but it's early, there's still time.

I cross the room, seeing a woman standing behind the bar, a hard look on her face as she slides a beer down the bar top. The guy she's serving catches it before it falls off, and I have to control my squeal of delight. I stop this side of the bar, waiting to be acknowledged, because you know, I wanna make a good impression. Gotta have good manners if I want to get this job.

The woman behind the bar grabs a dish rag and wipes the

bar top as she makes her way to me. "You must be John's new kid."

I nod my head enthusiastically causing her to let out a chuckle as she chunks the rag in the corner. "I'm Ell."

"You seem a little young. How old are you?"

Don't panic. I planned for this and used a little bit of magic to conjure up a fake I.D. making me twenty-one. I tell her my age, and when she seems unsure, I pull the I.D. from my back pocket, flipping the plastic over for her to see. She grabs it, looking it over, and seeming satisfied, she hands it back to me.

"Alright, hun. Tonight's an audition," she says as she hands me a tray with a money caddy attached. "That means ya only make tips. But if ya do a good job, then we'll get some paperwork done before ya leave tonight."

"Yes, ma'am," I nod.

Ohhh, look at me being all respectful and shit.

"Never call me ma'am, just Peg," she says before motioning to the rest of the room. "You're working on your own tonight. Stay on top of drink orders or the customers'll give ya hell."

My eyes widen slightly because I'm not sure what kind of hell. Also, I have a different perception of hell than humans do, so her statement is kind of unnerving. I open my mouth to ask a question, but seeing a middle-aged man at a table of four raise his hand and wave, I decide I better not make him wait. I rush over with a beaming smile on my face, and ask him for his order. Gotta earn those tips.

After I've got it, I turn back to the bar, repeating it over and over. Two Bud Lights, one long island iced tea, a rum and coke, and four shots of tequila. Or wait, was that two rum and cokes and three shots of tequila? Damn it. No, it was four. I got this.

I repeat the order to Peg, and while she makes it, I turn around, pressing my back to the bar and propping my elbows on the top. I scan the room, eyeing the drinks on each table to make sure everyone is still good. My eyes make it back to the pool tables, and oh my God. What the hell is that? I guess I should say, *who* the hell is that?

Red alert. Red alert. Hot piece of man candy at nine o'clock. Someone get a hose in here, there's a four-alarm hottie in the building. Okay, I'll stop, but *damn*. How did I miss him the first go 'round?

I'm so engrossed in checking him out, I totally miss that Peg is practically hollering my name. I sort of hear her, but it's not until she slaps me with the rag in the shoulder that I make it back down to Earth. I spin around, nearly tripping over my own feet, and grab the tray before rushing off, hearing her chuckle behind me. Making it back to the table of four, I hand the drinks out, but I'm struggling to pay attention. All I want to do is stare at Hottie McHotterson for the rest of my life. His arms are crossed tightly against his bulging chest, and it's obvious he works out. I can think of a few ways he can use me for a workout. Get it? Yeah you do.

My eyes slowly descend from his chest, but I'm jolted back to reality when the customer waves a wad of money in my face and tells me to keep the change. I thank him before turning and heading back to the bar. Setting my tray down, I pay for their drinks and realize the guy gave me a seven-dollar tip. Dang. That was easy. I'm kind of excited. No, I'm a lot excited. I've never actually earned money before. I've always just had everything given to me. This is fun.

Now, back to the hottie.

I make a lap around the room, taking a few more orders, but what I'm really doing is soaking in every single detail about the man I might be in love with. He is the definition of a tall drink of water. He has dark-brown hair, almost like chocolate, and it's the perfect amount of messy. His eyes are a pale blue, and he has the cutest lickable dimples. He's brawny, and he reminds me of a hot version of the paper towel guy, and yes, we know all about the paper towel guy in Fay. He even has on a red plaid button-up flannel shirt with a pair of worn black jeans. And his ass. He's only turned around once when he went to check on something in the back, but my, oh my. I just wanna squeeze it. And rub it. And...You get the idea. I want it. Mommy like.

Okay, that was creepy. I'm just saying, he's hot. And the best part is, he works here too. My guess is security, although no one has actually told me that. But when two guys got in an argument earlier, he stepped in, big bulging muscles and all. He also went back in the back and talked to Peg several times, so yeah, I'd say this is the best job ever. I just have to pray I nail this audition so that someday the hottie can nail me. Yes, I know that was cheesy. Ask me if I care.

A customer hollers for me, rudely interrupting yet another perusal, and with a huff, I make my way over. He gives me this long drink order that no real person could ever remember before shooing me away like a dog. So rude. I roll my eyes once my back is turned and rush back to the bar praying I get this right. I rattle off everything I think the guy said, and while Peg does give me an odd look, she doesn't question me as she moves to get started. It takes her a few minutes, but she does get it done, and I load my tray up. I carefully zig-zag through the room, slide up to the far table along the wall, and start setting drinks down.

The guy immediately starts yelling, and I haven't even finished setting them out. "Are you stupid or something!?!"

"No...sir," I stutter, setting two bottles of beer down. "Did I mess something up?"

He turns to one of his buddies, an evil smirk on his face. "*Did she mess something up?*" The sarcasm is real with this one. "Did she mess up? Are you fucking kidding me, *bitch*?"

I open my mouth to apologize, but before I can, Mr. Sexy Shmexy snatches the guy by the collar before slamming him against the wall.

Whoa, down girl.

My future baby daddy's jaw clenches, fury etched in his features. "You kiss your momma with that mouth, *Brandon*?"

Their noses are practically touching, and if I was Brandon,

I'd be pissing my pants right about now. He tries to stutter out a response, but hot stuff pushes him against the wall harder, refusing to let him speak.

"I think you've had enough tonight. Go home." The last few words are said through a growl, and I'll be honest, I'm totally turned on right now. Is that weird? Well, if it is, I don't care.

Brandon's feet hit the floor, and without a word he races out of the bar. His friends aren't far behind, although one of them at least has the decency to chunk a few twenties on the table for the drinks they ordered. It's a good thing too, because not only can I not afford to pay for these, I could also really use a drink and Brandon owes me one.

Stud Muffin turns to me, his gruff features lightening just slightly. "You okay?"

"That depends. What's the policy on drinking on the clock?"

He lets out a deep chuckle before picking up two shots of tequila. He hands one to me and keeps the other for himself. "I'm Blake."

"Ell."

The slightest of smiles dares to peek out from the corner of his kissable lips as he clinks his glass to mine and says, "Bottoms up."

I don't waste any time downing the yellowish liquid, and I'm not embarrassed when I grab a second shot and down it too. Blake gives me a small smile before turning and walking back to his normal station, and I hate to see him leave, but I *love* to watch him go. You get it.

I sigh. I think this is the start of a very *hot* friendship.

ROLLER-COASTER RIDE

I got the job, y'all! As soon as the bar closed that first night, Peg had called me over, checked to make sure my money caddy was right, and offered me the job. I'm officially a waitress at The Oasis four nights' a week, and she said she might even call me in if need be, so there's the potential for more hours. Look at me totally killin' it at being an ordinary human.

I worked Friday, Saturday, and Sunday of last weekend without a hitch, and then Monday, Tuesday, and Wednesday I helped Peepaw out around the ranch, and Meemaw out in the kitchen. I'd offered to give them some of my tips, but they'd told me to keep them for now until I got on my feet. Did I mention I love it here? Being human is awesome. Sure there are a few a-holes, but for the most part, I couldn't have ended up in a better situation.

As great as it's been, I've spent the last couple days waiting for the other shoe to drop. I sort of thought my dad or the royal guards would've showed up by now and drug me home. But now that it's Thursday and I'm walking in to work my shift, I'm starting to think I might have gotten away with this. It's not like I'm going to stay here forever. No, I just want a little *me* time. I want to experience things without the guards or my dad hovering over me. No matter where I went in Fay, there's no way I could have done that. They would have been all over me within a matter of hours. But here, on Earth, finding me will be like trying to find a needle in a haystack, and that's assuming he even thinks I'm on Earth. Most likely, he thinks I'm traipsing around Fay with Tab or some other friend. I really should've told Tab so she could've covered for me, but oh well. There's no way she would've let me come alone and have all this fun without her. Of course, knowing her she wouldn't think having a job and responsibilities was fun, but that's the difference in me and her. I'll never have to work a regular job, she will. I mean yes, being the queen will be a lot of work, but it's just not the same, ya know?

I make it to the front door of the bar, but before I can reach for the handle it swings open, Blake appearing in all his splendid glory. He gives me a nod and I step in, scanning the room to see how busy we are. My eyes land on a table of three and I falter. Shit. Fairies. I gotta get out of here. I turn back to the door, but Blake is blocking my path. I can't just bail. Maybe I could say I'm sick. But then that would leave Peg without a waitress tonight and I just don't want to do that. Damn it.

"Ell, you okay?"

Blake's husky voice startles me, and I fail to come up with something to say. Instead, I open and close my mouth, no doubt looking like a damn fish before turning and sprinting for the bathroom.

Inside there are a couple stalls, and I check each one to make sure I'm alone. Once I'm sure the coast is clear, I lock the bathroom door from the inside before moving to stand in front of the sink. Above the wet surface, I check out my features in the broken mirror. My lavender hair is still hidden under the glamour, although I could probably still pass for human even if I let it show. My pale skin is a darker shade than normal, and I toned down my emerald-green eyes just a touch. Everything seems to be working, but depending on how strong those three fairies are, they may be able to see right through my magic. Although, if they aren't Seelie or UnSeelie then I should be okay. But even if they can't see through my magic at what's underneath, that doesn't explain why they're here.

I got lucky that whatever glamour they're using is weak, and they failed to cover up the magical aura that surrounds a fairy, probably because they didn't expect another Fay to be here. If that hadn't been the case, I wouldn't have even realized they were fairies. That could've been really bad for me, especially if it turns out they're guards or UnSeelie. But I doubt they're guards. If guards showed up here, while they would definitely glamour themselves to fit in, I doubt they would sit down and grab a beer. I could be wrong, but I don't think so. But if that's the case, then who the hell *are* they?

A knock sounds at the door causing me to jump clean off the ground, my stomach doing a double flip. My hand flies to my chest. "Um, just a sec," I squeak. I assume it's a customer and they'll just have to wait, but when I hear Blake call through the door, I panic.

"Ell, you okay in there?"

"Uh, yeah. Emergency pee break," I call back, trying to keep the panic from my tone.

"Oh," he says, seeming surprised at my fake admission. "Okay well, I just wanted to check on you. You seemed spooked."

I shake my head even though he can't see me. "No. No, it was just a code red. I'll be out in a minute."

He says, "Okay," and I hear his footsteps retreat as I'm finally able to let out a sigh of relief.

I turn back to the mirror, scolding myself. Get it together, you idiot. I suck in a deep breath, splash a little water on my face, check my glamor five more times, and finally vacate the bathroom. Out front, I grab my tray from behind the bar, keeping my back to the fairies as long as I can. Maybe I can just avoid them all night. It sure would be helpful if it was crowded and we had a second waitress. If Liz was here I could make up some bullshit and get her to cover that table. As it is, I have no choice but to wait on them, unless I want to risk pissing them and Peg off. I just got this job and I can't afford to lose it.

I wipe down the bar and stools twice, stalling as long as I can, but eventually, I have no choice but to check on my customers. Chunking the rag behind the bar and grabbing my tray, I gradually work my way through the room, leaving the fairies for last. When I can't put it off another minute, I let my hair loose, allowing it to cover one eye. I trudge through the tables and stop a couple feet away being sure to keep my head down.

"Can I get ya'll anything?"

"Yeah, three Bud Lights," the tall, lanky one says, not even looking in my direction as he animatedly tells his friends a story.

I nod my head, not bothering to respond. I take two more small orders on the way back to the bar, and once I've spouted off the drinks like a pro, I turn, discreetly checking out the fairies' faces. I don't recognize any of them, but that doesn't mean anything. It's not like I know every single fairy. With their glamours up, I'm not even seeing the real them. For all I know they could be trolls or worse, orcs.

Checking to see that Peg is still working on the two long island iced teas I ordered, and seeing I have about two minutes left, I turn back to the fairies. I know I shouldn't be doing this, but I really need to see them without their glamour, so I have no choice but to add a little magic. I gather just a tiny amount from my magic-well, and fling it their way. I already knew they were weak, but it's proven when their glamours practically disintegrate before my eyes.

Fucking Elves. I'm pretty sure I mentioned how I feel about Elves. The only plus side is that there are very few Elves working in the guard, and I know most of them. So, that means these three being here is probably a random coincidence. I mean, it seems insane that three Elves walk into a bar, ha, that sounds like the start of a bad joke, anyway, that they just happened to stumble in here where a Seelie princess is hiding out, but whatever.

I'll take totally random for two-hundred, Alex.

***

The next hour goes by without any issues, other than when a group of girls celebrating their friend's birthday came rolling in. They'd definitely had some pre-cocktail-party cocktails. It had gotten so crowded that Peg had to call in another waitress, and now Liz and I flit around the room, dodging drunks and making bank. Seriously, I counted my tips a minute ago, and I'm already up to a hundred. That's a lot for this bar.

When there's a lull in the orders, Liz calls me over and slides a shot of tequila my way. We clink our glasses, downing it in one go and I immediately miss Tab. I wonder if I could get a message…

A big, sweaty body plows into me from behind and my shot-glass slips from my hands before shattering on the floor. My eyes jerk to Peg, worried she'll be mad, but she just hands me a broom and dustpan before turning to walk away.

"Sorry about that, beautiful," the offender says as I squat down to clean up the mess.

"Don't worry about it," I reassure him, glancing over my shoulder briefly. But as I move to turn back to the glass, something catches my eye. The guy who bumped into me is in fact one of the three Elves. The tall, lanky one, actually.

See, once you remove someone's glamour, it's really hard for the magic to work on you again. Which means even days from now if I run into them and they have a glamour on, I'll still be able to see the *real* them. That includes the very obvious UnSeelie mark on this one's wrist. I don't know how I missed it earlier, but I definitely did. There's no doubt in my mind this guy is an UnSeelie and his friends are too. UnSeelie and Seelie do *not* hang out and, for the most part, UnSeelie don't hang out with non-marked fairies either. So that means if he's got a mark, his friends do too. On top of that, they're Elves, and I know I've mentioned this, but Elves are the snobs of the fairy world, so that makes it even less likely they'd be hanging out with randos.

I realize I've been staring too long when the Elf says, "See something you like?"

Before I can utter a response, Blake moves swiftly through the crowd, pushing the drunk birthday girl off him as he approaches. "We got a problem here?" He towers over the Elf, his fists clenching and unclenching at his side.

The Elf raises his hands in surrender as he takes two steps back. "No problem here, man. I was just apologizing to the pretty lady."

Blake doesn't respond, so the Elf takes that as his cue to leave, rejoining his friends at the far table as I turn back to finish cleaning up. I sweep the last few shards of glass into the dustpan, walking to the trashcan by the wall and making sure to clean all the little pieces off after dumping the larger ones. I hand the broom and dustpan back to Peg, and move to retrieve my tray, but I don't have to go far because Blake has brought it to me like the night in shining armor that he is.

I'm pretty sure tiny hearts flash in my eyes as I take the tray from him with a smile. "Thanks."

He gives me a respectful nod before leaving me with Liz. I watch him walk away because it's the best view in the house, and I wince when Liz elbows me in the side, pulling my attention back to her.

"Um, excuse me, rude." I raise a brow before giving her a nudge in return.

Liz giggles, giving the room her back so no one will hear her. "So, you've got it bad for Hottie McHotterson."

"Oh my God, that's what I call him too." We both giggle, but I suck in a shocked breath when I realize I just admitted to having it bad for Blake. But honestly, I'm not fooling anyone. I haven't exactly been subtle, what with all the ogling I do each night.

"Okay, so warning," she says in a conspiratorial whisper, her hand cupped around one side of her mouth to block her words. "His last girlfriend really dicked him over. So I'm not sure where he's at right now up here." She taps her temple twice before giving me a playful nudge. "But, if the constant staring is any indication, I'd say he's into you too. So, because I'm awesome, I'll invite some people over Monday night, including you and Blake. It's a lot easier to get to know someone with a little less noise and a whole lot of alcohol."

"Really?" I suck in a breath because it would be nice to get to talk to him about something non-work related. Plus, I'd love the chance to make some new friends. Liz and I have spent time together at work, but that's it, so while I'd call her a work friend, that would be the extent of it. I'm not used to being a loner. I've always had Tab around. I don't like the feeling of being alone. I'm capable, I just don't like it.

She grabs a slip of paper and thrusts it at me. "Write your number down and I'll text you the details."

I have to pull back the squeal of excitement that tries to burst out as I jot down my number and hand it back to her. Thank God I used last weekend's tips to buy a cheap cell phone. Shoving the slip in her apron, she turns, and with a flip of her dirty-blonde hair she heads to take an order. I leave the bar to do the same, but my eyes land on Blake, and I can't help the grin that splits my face when I see he is, in fact, staring.

Finally, this is about to get juicy.

***

Thirty minutes till closing and I thought I was going to make it through this night without any major issues. Boy was I wrong. It was last call, and I'd made it to every table except the last one where the three fairies still sat. I was hoping if I took my sweet-ass time, I might not even have to go back there again. Unfortunately, I'm too good at my job.

I'd taken the three ass-hat's drink order, same as before, and zipped to the bar to grab the three Bud Lights. When I returned, a-hole number one, the same one who bumped into me earlier, decided to take his time handing me the money so his friends could hit on me.

I mean, *eww*.

Just to give you some perspective, one of them used the age old line, *'if I could rearrange the alphabet, I'd put U and I together'.* I mean, seriously? Kill me now.

After two more pick-up lines, tall and lanky fumbled with the money, acting as if he planned to hand it to me, but instead dropped it on the floor so I would have no choice but to bend over and pick it up. Classic, right?

I bent over, grasping the money, and that's when I heard and felt a slap on my ass. That's right, this mother-f'er slapped me on the ass. I turned around, ready to give him a massive piece of my mind, but it was too late.

So that is how I ended up standing here, unable to move because I can't stop watching Blake beat the ever loving shit out of three fairies. I know there has to be something wrong with me, but I have never, and I do mean *never*, been so hot and bothered in my whole life. I can't even find the strength or the want to step in and try to break it up. I may or may not have yelled, "*Beat his ass, Blake!*" I'm not even ashamed.

Now, fairy number one is unconscious on the floor, while two and three try their best to keep from getting murdered. Ohhhh, *damn*. Okay, number two is out, slumped over on top of his friend.

I watch as Blake gets in a good hit to the third fairy's temple, and I feel my body temperature rise again, but it isn't what you think. A glow appears around the fairy's right hand, and while no normal human would be able to see it, I damn sure can. He's going to use magic right here in the middle of The Oasis for all the world to see. The humans might not be able to see the glow, but they'll damn sure know something is up, depending on what this clown is planning. I can't let that happen. Not just because Blake might be seriously hurt, but because my cover may be blown. Fairy magic leaves behind an energy stream, so if my dad is looking for me, this could lead him right to me. I might have the ability to clean up my own stream, but not someone else's. I think it's possible, but I sure don't know how to do it. So, my only option is to use magic before he does.

The fairy's hand turns a brighter blue, and I take a quick look around. No one is looking at me, so as Blake rears back for another punch, I swirl my magic in a discreet circle. The minute Blake's fist connects with the fairy's nose, I wiggle my fingers.

Just so you know, the finger wiggle is just for show.

My magic hits the fairy in the nose at the same time Blake's fist connects, and with the exception of a sparkle that most humans can't see, and the fairy's eyes turning lavender with my magic for a split second, no one is the wiser when he slumps forward landing in Blake's outstretched arms.

I let out a sigh of relief as Blake dumps his body on the concrete floor, his head landing with a sickening crunch. Peg appears, slapping Blake on the back and congratulating him for a job well done. I'm a little queasy, the act of magic superseding the lust that had consumed me just moments ago. I would really like to get back to the lust if you don't mind. Having to be discreet with my magic, and trying to simultaneously clean up the energy stream has left me with a bout of magic sickness and I don't like it.

An arm slips around me and I jump, but turning and seeing Liz's concerned eyes, I calm almost instantly. "Sorry, I didn't mean to scare you," she says, giving me a squeeze. "You okay?"

I nod, not wanting to risk talking just yet as my eyes connect with Blake's. He mouths, 'you okay' and I mouth, 'yes', before allowing myself to be pulled away by Liz. She guides me to the bathroom before grabbing a few paper towels and wetting them under the constant stream of water in the leaky sink. I'm not sure what that's for. I didn't get into a fight, Blake did. I'm fine. But as she begins to dab under my eyes, I glance in the mirror and realize I must have been crying at some point. I'm not sure how that happened. Tonight has been a real roller-coaster ride.

STAGE FIVE CLINGER

Last night sucked. That's all.

By the time Liz and I had come back out of the bathroom, the fairies were gone and most of the mess had been cleaned up. Since it was closing time anyway, Liz and Peg had felt bad enough for me that they sent me home, offering to handle closing themselves. I had really appreciated that because I was not right after the encounter and the magic sickness. I'd been even more grateful when Blake insisted on walking me out. We had walked side-by-side to the far side of the parking lot where Peepaw had been waiting to take me home. Of course, I had to explain to Peepaw what happened and he had not been a happy camper. Although, he calmed down quite a bit when Blake explained the three assholes had been, and I quote, 'Taken care of'. He'd driven me home and practically tucked me into bed as if I was a small child. I wasn't complaining though. It made me feel cared for; loved.

The compassion and caring had not stopped with that though. This morning Meemaw had made a full breakfast spread. All of my favorites. And then afterward she'd told me to hurry and get dressed because we were going shopping in town. Despite knowing I really couldn't afford to buy much, I didn't refuse the trip.

The ride to town has been filled with laughter as I ride between Meemaw and Peepaw. The truck bounces as we round a corner before pulling into an empty spot outside the drug store. Peepaw hops out, rushing around to the other side before opening the door for the two of us. I just love how gentlemanly the men of this town are. I don't know if it's just this town, or the south in general, but I could get used to this.

"Ladies," he says, offering Meemaw and I each an elbow.

We each take his offered arm, allowing him to escort us in the drug store. We head to the back of the store, where he leaves us in the, as he calls it, 'ladies things', before walking away. It's just the makeup department. I swear, that man kills me.

Meemaw makes a bee-line for the cold cream, picking out her favorite kind as I search for a new lipstick for Monday night. I find one called cherry rush, and checking it on my wrist, I decide it will do just fine. My eye catches on a lip gloss with a similar name, and with a quick sniff, I figure, why not? On the off chance I do get lucky, now my lips will taste divine. You're welcome, Blake Black.

I find Meemaw three aisles over looking at the pantyhose and I giggle. I didn't even realize women still wore those things. Kind of seems like an outdated notion, but who am I to judge. She holds a pair of nude thigh-highs up, asking for my opinion.

"You know, you could just let those fine legs of yours show," I offer with a sly grin.

She swats me with the hose, feigning shock as she metaphorically clutches her pearls. "I would never...Now, which pair?"

I shrug. "The darker pair, I guess."

"Yes," she agrees with a nod. "These'll do just fine."

Twenty minutes later, we're checked out and headed to the florist. Meemaw said she needed some flowers for the dinner table, so while she and Peepaw pick some out, I decide to wait out front. My back leans against the brick wall as I eye the street. There aren't a lot of people out, but a few move here and there. Every once in a while a car passes by, but before long, I'm bored, and decide to take a walk around the block. Pulling my phone from my back pocket, I aimlessly walk while stalking Blake on social media. Night before last I ended up down a rabbit hole doing this very thing, and come to find out, Blake has made only five posts since 2016. And honestly, I'm pretty sure two of those were made by his ex-girlfriend, who is hot by the way. Like ridiculous hot. It's a good thing she's a terrible person and cheated on Blake, because otherwise it wouldn't be fair to the rest of us.

Not looking up, I turn a corner as I scroll through the three pics on his page. I pull up his profile picture, completely engrossed in his amazing eyes when my body slams into something hard.

"Sorry." I don't glance up as I sidestep the stranger.

"Ell?"

My eyes dart up, connecting with the beautiful blue eyes I'd just been staring at on my screen. Only now they're right in front of me. My phone is on, his picture up and I'm pretty sure he saw. Assuming the smirk on his face right now isn't unrelated. Oh, it's totally related.

"Uh." I don't know how to recover from this. "Hi?" I said it like a question. Why did I say it like a question? Complete idiot.

"Hey." He slides both hands in his pockets as his eyes drop to my screen again. "Doin' a little research?"

Dear, God.

"What? No. I...I was just gonna send you a friend request." Nice save, moron. I should just turn around and walk away now before this gets any worse. If I was smart, I'd go back to Fay and act like none of this ever happened.

"Oh yeah? Well, I don't really do the social media."

"*The social media*?" I question, giving him a hard time, but he clearly doesn't get it because he just nods a confirmation.

"Yeah, I prefer to talk to people in person." He winks at me, and I swear I just died. Seriously, can we get a medic in here?

I'm struggling to breathe as someone calls his name out by the street. He looks between them and me, and I get the distinct impression he doesn't want to leave. Or I could just be grasping.

"Well, I better go," he says, hesitantly.

I nod because I still can't speak, and without another word he leaves. I'm frozen to my spot, pissed off that I'm such a dumbass. Finally, I storm toward where Peepaw left the truck, praying they're ready to leave. I'm never going to live this down, and I just want to drown my sorrows in a big bowl of strawberry ice-cream.

Making it to the truck, I see they aren't back yet, so with a huff, I lower the tailgate and hop on. I practically slam my phone down. After all, it's my phone's fault I'm in this mess in the first place. The one time it doesn't turn off in two seconds flat. I swear.

I scan the street, looking for Meemaw and Peepaw, but I find Blake instead. He's talking to two guys across the street, his hands shoved in his pockets. He glances my way, catching me staring like a total creeper and I quickly look away. I just thought this couldn't get any worse. I've never been so wrong in my life.

I look anywhere but in his direction as I hear a truck door shut followed by a truck engine revving up. Out of my periphery, I see the truck backing out of a spot across the street and in front of me, and I swear I try not to look. But clearly I'm a glutton, because no matter how hard I try, I just can't help it. Also, the truck is just stopped in the middle of the road right in front of me. It's like whoever it is, is begging me to look.

Fine.

My eyes cast up, connecting with Blake as he rolls his window down. "I'll see you at work, Ell." He winks again, and I wave.

"Yeah, see ya."

***

Well, that was mortifying. I mean, I think we kind of pulled it out there at the end, but damn. You'd think I'd never spoken words to a member of the opposite sex before. I've spent all afternoon freaking out about him catching me being a total stage five clinger. Just a heads up, do not social media stalk a boy in broad daylight. Seriously, you're just asking to get caught. You leave that shit for 3:00 a.m., in bed and under the covers with the lights out like a normal human being. I guess I'm not a normal human being, but I feel like that's a universal truth.

My strawberry ice-cream melts in the bowl in front of me as I play over our encounter a million times. If I was a sane person, I'd just go back to Fay and act like none of this ever happened. I think the only reason he even spoke to me there at the end was because he felt sorry for me. I mean, I didn't detect pity in his tone, but what else could it be? Then again, I could just be spiraling.

A burst of wind pushes me as I kick my legs back and forth on the swing. Setting my bowl down, I slip my shoes back on, prepared to head back inside when an unusual noise catches my attention. I turn, trying to gage where it's coming from, but I don't hear it again. Shaking it off, I grab my bowl and head for the porch, but as soon as I get one foot on the first step, I hear it again. My head shoots to the right, certain that's where it came from.

Meemaw steps through the screen door, scaring the shit out of me. "Everything okay, hun?"

"Huh? Oh, yeah. I was just gonna go for a jog to burn off all that ice cream." That's a lie. I do *not* do exercise.

"Well, alright. Give me your bowl. I'll rinse it out for ya."

"I can do it," I offer.

She shakes her head, snatching the bowl from me and turning back to the door. I don't wait for her to get inside, instead I head toward the wooded area to the right. It takes me a while to get across the open pasture, but as soon as I step under the canopy, I hear the noise again. The bad part is, I know that sound.

"Wisps."

Why the hell are will-'o-the-wisps here? They've been banned from entering the Earth Realm for over a hundred years. In fact, my mom's dad was the one who banned them. I don't remember why, but it had something to do with Ireland and it wasn't good.

Wisps are a fairy whose original purpose was to lead humans to their greatest destiny. Unfortunately, there's such a thing as free will, even for fairies, and centuries ago, they decided they didn't like their job, so they just stopped. After that they did nothing but cause mischief. They are completely immature if you ask me. Those tiny little blue bastards get on my nerves.

That doesn't stop me from continuing on as I hear the echoing call again. I stomp through the underbrush, having no clue where I'm going and half thinking I should go back. It's not like those fiery little shits will actually lead me to my destiny or anything.

Another five minutes passes, I'm just about to turn around when the tell-tale blue fire appears. It wavers and flits back and forth in a two-foot radius before jumping ahead, egging me on. This goes on for the better part of twenty minutes, and I'm really getting pissed.

I throw my hands up, letting out a shout. "Ugh! Why do you have to be so dramatic? Just tell me what you want already."

The call grows in volume and now it's all around me. Well now you've done it, Ell. You've really pissed them off. Also, it kind of freaks me out that wisps never travel alone. They're always in packs of at least fifty, even if you only see one. They're there. Oh, they're there.

One sounds near my ear and I jump a full foot, tripping over my own two feet on the way down. My head slams against a rock, stars bursting before my eyes. My vision is black on the sides as I try to drag myself to a sitting position. Propping my back against the base of a large pine tree, I feel my head for injury. My hand comes away dry, so at least there's that. But the damn wisps are gone, and all of this was for nothing.

My head lolls to the side, a plant I know well coming into view. "O. M. G. You bitches. How about you at least try to be a little more creative!" I shout the words, even though I can *feel* there's no one here but me.

Looking back to the crown of thorns growing oddly next to me, I'm pissed I came out here for this. But also, I'm pretty sure this plant isn't native to Texas, so that's odd. They grow widely in Fay, but I'm pretty sure I read somewhere that on Earth they only grow naturally in Madagascar.

I drag myself to my feet, trying to get my bearings. When I think I've figured out which direction the house is in, I storm forward, kicking rocks and chunking sticks as I go. I reach the pasture in no time, which is so weird, considering on the way it seemed to take a lot longer. Those damn wisps are probably responsible for that too. I mean, I guess I could read into this. Maybe they no longer wish to show humans their destiny, but they're willing to show me, a fairy, mine.

"Show the heir a crown of thorns," I mock, nearly back to the house. "We're soooo creative. We're wisps. Look at us."

Ugh.

I'm so ready for Monday.

THIRSTY BITCH

It's freaking Monday. That's right, all you haters out there that are like, '*Monday's suck*', well *you* suck. Monday's are fan-freaking-tastic. Well, they are if your new friend agreed to throw a small party just so you could get lucky with the sex-god security guard from your work. Yes, that was elaborate. I don't care because it's Monday. And even though I normally hate the act of getting dressed, I'm actually enjoying it right now. Why? Because it's Monday.

Humming a tune, I tug on my skin-tight white jeans, hopping around the room to get them up. I suck in a deep breath, and slip the snap in place before grabbing my black lace halter. Tying it behind my neck, I rush to the small dresser in my room, slapping on a little makeup followed by my new lipstick, and then finally a thin coat of the cherry gloss. My hair is naturally wavy, so I pull it to the side and secure it in a messy fishtail before reaching for my black heels.

With a final look in the mirror and topping off my glamour with a little extra magic, wouldn't want that to slip tonight, I leave my room to find Peepaw. I'm really hoping he doesn't mind dropping me off as long as I can get a ride home, but if not, Liz mentioned one of her friends lives close by and could pick me up on his way. I really don't want to do that, but I'll do what I have to do because it's Monday.

Searching the house twice, I don't find Peepaw or Meemaw, and I'm almost starting to worry. Those two took me in without even knowing me, and every day that passes we grow closer. They haven't let me pay them a dime in rent, even though I've offered, and while I do help out with chores, it's not like they really need me to do that. They're like the grandparents I always wanted, and when I have to go home, I'm really going to miss them.

I step out on the front porch, and the sight before me has my heart doing a little pitter-patter. The big oak tree out front gently sways in the breeze as Meemaw and Peepaw sit arm in arm in the attached swing. Be still my heart, *right now*. Peepaw says something too low for me to hear as I step off the front porch, and Meemaw laughs like a schoolgirl. As I approach, their attention turns to me, and they both wear welcoming smiles.

"Hey there, hun," Peepaw greets me, scooting over and patting the seat for me to join them.

I shake my head, but keep a smile plastered to my face. "No, actually, I made some friends at work, and they're all getting together to hang out tonight, so I was hoping you might drop me off. I can get a ride home because I might end up staying late."

"Who's house is it?" Meemaw asks the question with a motherly tone, and while some might find that annoying, I find it endearing.

"Liz...sorry, Elizabeth Baxter," I explain, hoping if they know her they don't have a problem with her or her family. I know how small towns work. Everyone knows everyone.

"Oh yes," Meemaw says with a bob of her head. "I know Liz and her family well. Good stock those Baxters'."

Peepaw agrees, "Good stock indeed." His thumb rubs back and forth on Meemaw's shoulder, and it has me wanting that someday. Not someone rubbing my shoulder necessarily, but someone that cares about me as much as these two do each other. They're just the best. Actually, to backtrack, yes, I want my shoulders rubbed. Like every single night.

I smile because these two are just two funny as I try to bring this back to my request. "So do you mind?"

"Actually," Peepaw sighs, "Meemaw and I were just about to head to bed, but why don't you take 'Ole Bessie."

Bessie is the truck; in case you were wondering. And boy

is it 'ole.

I just love how country I am already.

I squeal, clapping my hands in anticipation as I wait for Peepaw to toss me the keys. He reaches in his pocket, pulls out his Ford key chain with the keys attached, and pitches them end over end. I catch them like a pro before basically sprinting to the truck.

As I reach the door, I hear Meemaw shout, "Be home by two."

Aren't they just freaking adorable?

"Yes, ma'am," I holler as I swing the driver's side door open and hop in.

See, what I failed to mention is that I have never actually driven. Never had a need to. And what's worse, 'Ole Bessie is a standard. This could end very badly for me *and* Bessie.

I look at the stick protruding from the floorboard, and breathing in deep, I cram the key in the ignition and go for it. The engine grinds a little, a result of me turning the key too far, and I reach for the stick, ready to let off the brake. The gears grind as the truck lurches forward before dying. Well, that was embarrassing. Alright, second times a charm.

I don't look at Peepaw. I don't want to see the worry I know is written on his features as I start the truck once again. I contemplate for half-a-second using magic, but I'd have to use too much to cover my tracks and then I'd end up sick. I cannot be sick tonight, because it's Monday.

I try one more time putting it in first, and the only reason I even know to do that is by having watched Peepaw the last week or so. Bessie lurches forward again, but this time I give her a little more gas and she manages to even out. I don't let up, flooring it as I race down the driveway, dust kicking up in my rearview.

Best Monday ever.

***

Okay yes, Bessie died nine times on the way to Liz's house, and *I* nearly died twice, but who's counting? I'm here now, and I am *so* ready. I slam the door, brush my hands off on my thighs, and skip to the front door. Yes, I know I look ridiculous.

I knock twice, waiting only a half-a-second before a guy I don't know answers the door. He gives me a *what's-up* nod before turning and leaving me to enter on my own. Stepping inside, I close the door behind me before taking a minute to look around. The entryway leads to a well-lived in living room on the left, and a dining room with tons of food laid out on the right. I make a mental note to check the food out at some point before moving on to the rest of the house. I pass through the hall leading to a small kitchen where four people I haven't met before stand talking and drinking. I give them a friendly smile and, hearing music from the back, I assume that's where Liz must be. I step out the back door, the small but inviting yard filled with people, none of which I know. I *am* a people person, sort of, but I like to have my side-kick, a.k.a. Tab, with me. She's my back up, and not having her here right now has me feeling a little anxious and out of place.

A head splitting squeal sounds from my right and I turn. Liz races toward me, a red solo cup in one hand, the other flailing in the air in excitement. "Oh-m-gee. It's about time you got here." Liz throws her arm around me, dragging me down the last two steps and herding me to a group of three kegs in the far corner of the fenced in yard. She grabs a cup for me as I apologize and try to tell her about my near death experience, but it's clear she doesn't really care when she thrusts the full cup in my face before saying, "You need to catch up. I'm four in."

Let it be known, I will never turn down free beer or a challenge.

I take a tentative sip to test the flavor, but before I pull the cup away, Liz pushes the bottom, forcing me to down the whole thing. The frigid liquid dribbles down my chin, but I manage to get most of it down as I realize a group of guys are cheering for me. My cheeks turn a light shade of pink as Liz snatches my cup, chunks it over her shoulder, and hands me a full one.

Oh, so she was serious about catching up. Got it.

I down that one too, and while my tolerance is fairly high due to the potency of fairy wine, if I keep this up, I'll be passed out by ten. Halfway through the third cup, Liz loses interest as a cute guy with a carrot top starts flirting with her. He looks like he's maybe in his late twenties, and it dawns on me I don't actually know how old Liz is. From her looks, I'd say maybe early twenties, but I'm also a horrible judge of age. One time I told a fairy how good she looked for being sixty, and she turned bright red and mumbled, "*I'm forty.*" Oops.

I watch the two of them flirt for a few more minutes, but a guy I recognize catches my eye and waves me over. Jayson's dad owns the hardware store and I met him yesterday when I rode to town with Peepaw. I'm happy to see someone I know, so I slip away from Liz and make my way over, nearly avoiding a head-on collision with a very drunk blonde girl. She also gives me a dirty look and flips me off. She looks oddly familiar, but I'm not sure where I would know here from, unless maybe she was with that birthday party at the bar. I don't think that's it though.

As I reach Jayson's side, it hits me. Holy shit, why is Blake's ex here?

She disappears into the house as Jayson says, "I didn't know you were friends with Liz." He nods in her direction.

Taking a sip of beer so I look cool, and trying to shake off the fact that Blake's super-hot ex-girlfriend is here, I bob my head. "Yeah, we work together at The Oasis."

"Cool."

"Cool," I parrot because I'm not sure what else to say. I swear I'm normally way cooler than this. O.M.G. Remind me to never say the word cool again. I'm just going to blame it on my run in with the ex. That really threw me off my game.

"So," he starts, seeming unsure of himself, "since you're new to town and all, I thought maybe I could take you out to dinner sometime."

My eyes widen. "Oh...um..."

He seems hurt, his face falling as he tries to recover. "It's no big deal. I was just trying to be nice."

Now *my* face falls, but I don't have time to comment because Liz is barreling toward me. She grabs me by the wrist as she gives Jayson a dirty look before pulling me away from the small crowd and around the corner. She takes two swallows of her beer as if it might get away from her before saying, "I just saw Blake through the kitchen window. It's time to do *yo* thang."

My heart rate kicks up a notch, excitement coursing through me, but I don't know what to say or how I should act. Are Blake and I friends? Should I just go in and start up a conversation or should I do what I want, and throw myself on him as soon as I see him? I talk a big game, but we all know I'm not going to go with the latter. And then there's the issue of the ex.

"Oh my god, you're so cute when you're nervous," Liz giggles, a burp slipping past her lips. She doesn't even apologize, which is fine by me, as she adds, "Okay, let's go." She tugs me, but I pull back causing her to stumble. She turns to me with a questioning look.

"I think I ran into Blake's ex, literally."

She nods. "Yeah, Ava's here. She's totally plastered."

"Why are you acting like this isn't a big deal?"

She rolls her eyes at me and says, "Because it isn't. Listen Ell, this is a small town. There is no getting away from our exes, but you have nothing to worry about. Yes, she's a bitch, but that's the point. She really did Blake wrong, and there is no way he would go back to her." She pauses, taking a long swig from her cup. "Besides, he's totally into you. Now, stop stalling and come on."

Hand-in-hand, we slip around the corner, up the back-porch steps and into the kitchen. I take a deep cleansing breath, trying to shake off my nerves as Liz pulls us over to two guys talking in the corner. She's at least acting casual as we both pretend like we're interested in the conversation. Liz strikes me as a zero filter kind of gal, so I'd half assumed as soon as we stepped foot in the kitchen she'd go straight to Blake and say, "*Ell wants to fuck you*". Thank God she didn't, unless of course his answer was okay, in that case I would have been good with it.

Liz lets out a maniacal laugh, and I don't even think she knows what these two guys are talking about. They give her an odd look as I lower my head, not wanting to be associated with her current level of crazy. It might actually be all for nothing because my back is to the rest of the room, so I'm not sure if Blake is even paying attention to us. Wouldn't that be embarrassing?

Liz laughs again, throwing her head back and tugging me in close. "Oh Todd, you are so fucking funny. You just kill me." She's talking super loud and I cringe, slowly slipping my body out of her grasp. Todd shakes his head at her before casting his eyes over my shoulder causing me to turn.

Sweet, beautiful baby Jesus.

Blake stands propped against the small center island, one ankle kicked over the other like the sexy bad-ass he is. His messy brown hair sits in disarray on top of his head, and I wonder if he's one of those that spends two hours to get it to look like that or if he's just naturally sexy. Pretty sure it's natural.

My eyes have already cast up and down his body twice, landing on his inviting blue eyes last. They're filled with mirth, and I realize he's been watching *me* checking *him* out for the last five minutes. I know I'm blushing, but when he nods his head toward the living room causing a giddy sensation to course through my body, I fail to hesitate in following him. Over my shoulder, I look to make sure Liz sees me leaving, and when she gives me a smirk and a cheesy thumbs-up, I know we're good.

I turn the corner, stepping into the living room and find Blake propped against the back of the loveseat in much the same position as he was in the kitchen. A strand of hair slips across his eyes and he sweeps it back before taking a sip of something that's a yellowish-brown color. If I was to guess, it's probably whiskey, and I really wish I was drinking that instead of beer.

I slide up against the loveseat, propping my hip against the back, my arms crossed nervously against my chest. I'm not sure why I'm so nervous. It's not like we're about to do the deed.

I mean that would be nice, but I'm not a total slut. I'll at least make him buy me dinner first. Yes, I know I'm being a thirsty bitch right now. Ask me if I care.

"So," Blake says, his voice low and sexy. "I see Liz managed to drag you to one of her famous parties."

I quirk a brow in his direction. "Famous?"

He returns my raised brow before explaining. "Famous for flowing alcohol and excessive public hook-ups. It's a small town, so pretty much everyone has hooked up at some point."

That surprises me. "When you say hook up…"

It's a valid question. Hooking up has different meanings depending on who you're hanging with. Some might say it's just making out or kissing someone, while others might be talking about, well, you know.

"I mean, *hooking up*." He puts extra emphasis on the hooking up part before pumping his eyebrows twice. "As I said, it's a small town. Not much else to do but get drunk and…"

He doesn't finish his sentence as I nearly choke on my own spit at his suggestiveness. I practically hack up a lung, and I'm mortified when he starts beating his hand against my back. What am I, a toddler?

When I finally get it together he asks, "You okay?"

I'm too embarrassed to speak so I just nod as he thrusts his drink toward me. I take it without hesitation, swallowing a small sip before confirming it is whiskey. Good whiskey too, and I really wish I had my own. I take a second sip before trying to hand it back but he shakes his head and tells me to keep it. I don't know why that gives me a warm fuzzy feeling, but it does, and I thank him before downing the whole glass. This is the liquid courage I needed.

He chuckles, his whole chest bouncing with the action as I swallow the last drop. "So…I heard Jayson asked you out."

"Damn," I remark. "This *is* a small town. That was like twenty-minutes ago."

We both share a laugh, but then his features turn serious. "So, you're gonna go out with Jayson then."

It's spoken more as a statement than a question, and I shake my head. "Actually, I never got the chance to answer. Liz drug me off before I could."

He seems surprised by that or pleased, it's hard to tell under his somewhat gruff features.

"Well, for the record, *I* would be disappointed if you did."

"What do you mean?" I ask, cocking my head to the side and wishing I had another drink.

He stands from his perch, holding his hand out and waiting on me to take it. When I slip my hand in his, he says, "*I* would be disappointed if *you* went out with Jayson. Don't get me wrong, Jayson is a nice guy, but…" His words trail off as I blush a deep-crimson. I hope I'm not reading into his meaning because that would be a total let down.

My core clenches at his admission as he guides me almost lovingly through the front of the house and back to the kitchen. He takes the empty glass from my hands, grabs another from the cabinet, and fills both nearly to the brim with whiskey. He hands one back to me, and then we clink glasses softly before throwing back a big swallow.

I lean back against the counter, trying to look relaxed. He props his ass against the island across from me, and the eye contact is getting intense. I need to think of something to say to break the silence, but the only thing I can think of is, "So I ran into your ex-girlfriend."

His eyes go wide and he sputters out a cough. I mentally slap, pinch, and kick myself. I can't believe I even said that. There is something seriously wrong with me. I've only known Blake for a few days, and I'm not even sure what to call us. He might just think of us as work acquaintances, which means I'm some stranger bringing up his ex.

He takes a swig of his whiskey before finally clearing his throat. "Yeah, I ran into her too." He pauses, an odd expression slipping over his features. "Wait, how do you know my ex?"

Well, fuck. Oh, I don't know. Maybe because I stalked your page, and then your exes, and then your exes' mom, best friend, and Aunt Sheila. I even know that Ava's grandma just celebrated her 87th birthday at Disneyland. I know all the things, but I can't tell him that so instead, I lie.

"Well, I didn't until earlier," I say. "She ran into me, gave me a go-to-hell look, and then flipped me off. Liz told me who she was."

"Ahh," he says, believing me. "Yeah, she can be a lot to handle, especially drunk." He finishes off the last of his whiskey before crossing to the bottle, and pouring us both three fingers, he adds, "But, I don't really want to spend the night talking about my ex." He props his hip against the counter next to me as I turn to face him more fully.

"Oh. Well, what did you wanna talk about?" I ask, intrigued at this very amazing turn of events.

"You."

I'm officially giddy. Fuck Ava. He doesn't want to talk about *her*, he wants to talk about *me*. That's right, because I'm awesome and she's not.

We spend the next hour getting to know each other, and as he pours me yet another glass of whiskey, my nose starts to tingle which is a tell-tale sign I'm buzzed and on my way to drunk, but I don't care. If I'm too drunk to drive, then I'll get someone to take me or stay the night here and just call Meemaw and Peepaw so they don't worry.

I'm not gonna worry about that or anything else. Tonight, I'm gonna cinch the deal.

RULE BREAKING

Okay, so I didn't cinch the deal, whatever. I did, however, spend the rest of the night with Blake. We drank, we laughed, and we got to know each other. He was more than sweet, and I really like him. Like really, really like him. Like not just want him to rip my clothes like, but like, like-like. I mean, I was a goner when at ten till two I started freaking out about being late for curfew and knowing I was too drunk to drive, and he offered to give me a ride. I'd been worried about leaving Bessie, but he'd promised to come get me first thing this morning so I could go pick the truck up and bring it back. Like I said, like-like.

    When I woke up this morning, I woke with a smile on my face, and it had only gotten bigger when Meemaw slipped in my room carrying a tray piled with breakfast foods. She'd said she thought I might need this since she figured I had a hangover, and then told me to down the green liquid in the glass. '*A family hangover secret*', she'd said. Thirty minutes later, any remnants of a hangover were gone, and I was really feeling like Meemaw needed to market that shit. *Meemaw's Hangover Elixir. Meemaw's Hair Of The Dog. Meemaw's Post Bad Decisions Remedy.* Whatever. We'll figure it out.

    Anyway, I'd left that for another day when I realized it was already 9:30 and Blake was supposed to pick me up at 10:00. I'd rushed through getting dressed, but took a little extra care with my makeup knowing who I was about to see, and then rushed past Peepaw and out to the porch.

    Now as I sit on the front steps waiting, my hands wrapped around my knees, pulling them tightly to my chest, I see a plume of dust at the end of the drive and I know he's almost here. My heart skips a beat at the thought of seeing him again, and when he pulls up and gets out instead of honking, my stomach fills with butterflies.

I know I have a stupid grin on my face as he approaches the porch with a, "Mornin'."

"Good morning," I return, slipping my hand in his waiting one.

He helps me off the few steps, moving us quickly to his waiting truck, but when I hear the screen door creak open and Peepaw holler, "Now wait just a minute there," Blake and I turn, his hand freezing on the passenger door handle. "Where do you two think you're goin'?"

I almost laugh, but his tone and expression tell me he's serious. "I left Bessie at Liz's last night since I drank, remember?"

"Yes well, be that as it may, missy, you don't leave with a boy without letting us know, and introducin' him."

My head jerks back in surprise. "Oh. I'm sorry. You guys know everyone in town. I guess I just assumed you two knew each other."

"We do," Peepaw confirms. "But that ain't the point."

He steps off the porch, approaching Blake and I as he attempts to look intimidating. It isn't working, at all. The hunch in his back makes it almost impossible, but he squares his shoulders and holds his head high.

Blake takes it in stride, extending his hand to shake as Peepaw returns the gesture. "Blake Black, sir. My daddy is Bucky Black, and my momma is Adele Black. I just promised to give Ell a ride to get your truck, sir. But, I was actually hoping after we return the truck, Ell might wanna have lunch with me."

A giddy sensation sweeps through me at how he slipped that in, and I hope Peepaw doesn't say no. I'm not sure what I would do if he did. I mean, they aren't my parents, but they are letting me live here, for free, I might add, and I want to be respectful. But I really, really want to go. I don't want to whine, but I will if I have to. I'm not above it. In fact, I'm not above getting on my knees and begging.

"Is that so…?" Peepaw trails off, turning to me to gage my reaction.

I attempt to give him a discreet, begging look, but I'm not sure if he gets it.

"Yes, sir," Blake says, looking at me. "That is, if she wants to."

"Well," John says a little loud, "do ya?"

I have to hold back the laugh at his behavior as I nod my head. "Yes, if that's okay with you." I can play along with what we've got going on here.

"Well, alrighty then. But you had a late night last night, so how about you be home by supper."

"Yes, sir," I confirm, turning back to the truck and moving to get away before this gets dragged out any further.

Blake opens my door, helping me up and in the passenger seat as I hear Peepaw yell from the front porch, "Bring your feller to supper if ya want!"

My cheeks turn a ridiculous shade of cherry as Blake shuts the door before crossing to the other side. He hops in, the truck starting with a shake and a roar, and I find myself hoping he'll come to dinner. I'm also oddly happy about what just went down with Peepaw. Most girls would have been mad at how he acted, given that he isn't even my dad, you'd think I would be too. But all I saw was a man who didn't even know me two weeks ago, but now he genuinely cares about me. I don't know what I'm going to do when I have to go home. I can't imagine how much I'll miss Meemaw and Peepaw. Maybe I could take them with me, but even as I think that, I know that isn't possible. Regardless, my chest swells with love for this little life I'm creating as Blake drives us toward town.

***

When we'd gotten to Liz's house, Bessie had been right where I left her, parked out by the street, the driver's side tires popped up on the curb. I think we've established that I can't drive. I'm working on it. That's just one thing I plan to master before my little vacay is over.

As soon as we'd gotten out of Blake's truck, Liz had come skipping out the front door and the two of them had proceeded to make fun of my lack of driving skills. It had all been in good fun though, and I let them rib me for a good ten minutes. We stayed for just a bit while Liz boasted about the carrot-top she'd hooked up with last night, and then Blake had followed me back home to drop the truck off. After that I'd jumped back in with him and the two of us had decided to have lunch at the little diner in town. The food had been amazing. There's nothing better than home-cookin' as far as I'm concerned.

Now my stomach is full as Blake leads me out the front door of the diner, his hand on the small of my back. Can we just take a moment? Let's just take a moment to talk about how sexy it is for a man to lead a woman in or out of a room by the small of her back. I can't be friends with anyone who disagrees.

Goosebumps sprout on my arms, a shiver coursing through my body as he opens the passenger door for me. After he gets in on his side and starts the truck up, I find myself disappointed when he heads for the dirt road that will lead us back to Meemaw and Peepaw's place or I guess, my place now too.

The radio plays a soft country tune in the background as the landscape drifts lazily past my window. Even though I wish he wasn't taking me home so soon, I'm still enjoying myself, and I feel like we had a great time over lunch. Kind of makes me wonder why he's so quick to drop me off. And does that mean he isn't coming for dinner?

I'm so immersed in my own thoughts, when Blake speaks, I nearly jump out of my seat, the seat belt cinching too tight. "I'm not really ready to take you home yet. Wanna go for a ride on backroads or I don't know, have you seen the lake yet? I could show you."

He sounds nervous, which has me nervous. "Yeah, the lake sounds fun."

A relieved smile slips across his lips as he rests his arm on the center console next to mine. Our hands are so close as we head down another dirt road, and I wish I had the balls to just hold his hand. I look straight ahead, trying not to think about how close we are, and when I feel his finger twitch against my thumb, my core does a double clench in response. When it happens again, I decide to be bold. I inch my thumb over just a bit, our fingers now fully touching. I guess my move gave him the confidence he needed, because without taking his eyes off the road, he slides his hand across the top of mine, gripping my fingers gently before entwining our fingers.

My nerves have my hands sweating, and I pray he isn't grossed out by it. "I'm sorry my hand is so sweaty." Better to just acknowledge it, I always say. That's a lie, I never say that.

"Is that *your* hand?" he questions, giving my hand a squeeze. "Because I thought it was mine."

He turns to look at me and we exchange a smile. I'm surprised he's so nervous. Blake isn't really as old as I am in fairy terms, but by human terms he has three years on me. Not to mention he's possibly the hottest man in the realm. I just can't imagine someone like him ever being nervous. What does *he* have to be nervous about? With his looks, he could have any woman he wants. There's no way he even has to try. I bet women are throwing themselves at him, and if he didn't live in this tiny town, he'd be raking in chicks. That thought has the tiny green jealousy monster rearing its ugly head, which is ridiculous. Not only do I not have the right, but it's not like he actually did anything wrong. I fully acknowledge women are crazy, regardless of the species.

The truck slows, pulling me from my thoughts as we come to a stop near a small gravel pull-off. The lake stands before us, the surface smooth as glass. Blake races around to my side, trying to let me out before I can do it myself, and I thank him as he slips his hand in mine, the two of us walking slowly toward the water's edge. I take a gulp of the fresh air, enjoying the feel of nature all around us. The birds singing just inside the tree line makes for a delightful date theme song. This is by far the best date I've ever been on, and I have no doubt, I'll never forget this day.

"It's beautiful," I say with a sigh, as Blake pulls me down to sit on a rotting log, a single daisy sprouting up through the cracks.

Blake doesn't comment. He just gives me a nod in agreement as he picks up a rock before attempting to make it skip across the water. The rock hits the surface, bouncing twice before sinking to the bottom. I cringe. He's doing it all wrong, but I'm hesitant to show him how. Some guys are weird about stuff like that.

I'm half River Nymph, and while this isn't a river, it *is* a body of water, so my affinity for water has my skin tingling. My instinct is to jump in and enjoy the cool feel of the liquid as it rejuvenates my magic, but I know I can't do that right now. It would be worse with a river, but even here, as soon as the water touched my skin, I'd be emitting a slew of magic. Enough that I'm not sure if I could control it or tamp it down, and since some humans can see *some* magic, especially strong magic, I just can't take that chance. Humans fear what they don't understand, and I'm not sure how Blake would feel if he knew who, or I guess, *what* I really am.

Blake skips a few more rocks, and as they each sink after only two bounces, I can't stop myself from giving it a try. Maybe if he sees me do it, he'll realize how wrong he is. I reach for a small, smooth stone and using my left hand, I give it a flick. The stone skims across the surface before skipping at least ten times and then disappears. I'm pleased with myself as Blake turns to me, a look of surprise on his face.

"What?" I shrug.

"Damn, showoff," he says, nudging his shoulder against mine playfully.

I just smile as I find another perfect stone and try again. This goes on for the better part of an hour as we take turns. I show him a few tricks of the trade, and by the time we're done, he manages to skip one eight times; a record for him.

Eventually, we both get bored with skipping stones, and

we lean back, enjoying the peaceful silence. I love how already we don't feel like we have to fill that silence. We both seem content with just being in each other's presence.

We sit like that for quite some time, until Blake breaks the silence when he casually puts his arm around me, and asks, "So, how do you like Electra so far?"

Let the small talk commence. "It's really kind of amazing. Plus, it doesn't hurt that I've met some amazing people, like Meemaw and Peepaw, Liz too."

He turns his head toward me, quirking a brow. "Is that all?"

"Yeah," I'm quick to reply. "I can't think of anyone else."

He lunges, digging his finger into my side, forcing a slew of giggles past my lips. I jerk back, falling on my side as he leans over me to get a better angle. He's relentless, even when I beg him to stop, and if I pee, I'll never forgive my bladder. Blake keeps it up as I try to wiggle away. He puts his hands down, trying to balance himself, but the loose gravel is not his friend. He falls forward, his body splaying out across mine. I'm positioned sort of on my back, but kind of on my side, and his front is pressed to mine. He pushes some of his weight off me, holding it up on the palm of his hands, and then we engage in a very intense stare down. It's one of those moments where the guy should most definitely kiss the girl, like in all the movies. But, apparently, I'm not in a movie, because he clears his throat before sitting upright and helping me to do the same. Our shoulders touch as we begin a five-minute awkward period where we each stare straight ahead and no one says a word.

Finally, Blake stands, wiping his hands off on the legs of his jeans. He reaches down, helping me to my feet and I assume we're leaving, but taking my hand, he leads me further away from the truck. We walk along the shoreline, the warm afternoon breeze whipping my hair around my face. The birds singing a tune above us makes the experience almost surreal, and I find myself praying this day never ends. We come to a small outcropping of trees, their branches towering high above us, and Blake stops just inside the canopy. His hand rubs nervously at the back of his neck as he slowly backs me against a tree. The bark cuts into my skin, keeping me in the present as I watch several emotions flit over his face.

"I like you," he says, surprising me. "Like a lot. I just got out of a really rough relationship though, so I wasn't looking for anything serious."

I can't help it when my shoulders sag in disappointment. I mean, I did say I just wanted to lose my v-card, so maybe he's still up for that. The problem is, now that I've gotten to know him, I don't just want a one-night stand. I want more than that. I feel drawn to him in a way I can't even explain. It's almost as if I was supposed to run away, end up in Electra, Texas, and meet Blake Black; as if we were supposed to be together. I know that sounds cheesy and weird, but as a fairy, when the universe speaks to you, you listen.

Blake seems to notice my disappointment as he takes a step closer, no more than an inch separating our bodies when he stops. "The problem is I like you too much for it to *not* be serious."

He moves one hand to rest above my head against the tree, and with the other, he absentmindedly slips his fingers through my hair as it drapes over my shoulder. The soft ministrations send tingles zipping across my scalp, and I suck in a breath, holding it.

"I had made a rule," he says, moving his fingertips up to my collar bone, ghosting his touch across my sensitive skin. "No serious relationships for a year."

His fingers are just a whisper against the skin of my neck and I'm melting. At this point, I don't give a shit if we're in a relationship or not, just kiss me already.

"But, I think I'm going to have to break that rule," he says.

A soft gasp escapes my lips and then he's moving. Not fast. No, he moves ever so slow. The time builds tension as my heart races. When his lips finally connect with mine, it isn't hard and aggressive. Instead, his lips make several brushing passes before they finally connect fully. His scent envelops me, cinnamon and maybe a hint of bonfire, and he uses his tongue to request entrance. I don't deny him, parting my lips and allowing his tongue to caress mine. His tongue toys with me, back and forth, the action ramping up my desire. I've kissed a lot of fairies in my life, but never have I experienced something like this. I can't decide if it's because he's a human and not a fairy, or if this is what it feels like when you kiss someone you really like for the first time.

My hands rest on his chest and I slide them up, securing them behind his neck. I entangle my fingers in his hair, scraping my nails softly on his scalp causing the softest of growls to vibrate through our connected mouths. I think that's both of our undoing, as he moves one hand behind my neck and the other slides down tugging the hem of my shirt. His thumb slides back and forth, the movement causing my shirt to ride up. When his thumb sneaks under the cotton fabric, the rough feel of the pad of his thumb rubbing circles on my side, I let out a whimper. I'm embarrassed for half-a-second, after all, we're only kissing, but when he growls again before pressing me harder to the tree, any embarrassment I may have had flies right out the window.

His hand under my shirt moves across my side ever so softly before coming to a stop on my bare lower back. He pulls his head back slightly, my disappointment ready to rear its ugly head, but when he sucks my bottom lip with a pop, I lose it. I give his hair a tug, my other hand pulling him closer; the friction I need seeming too far out of reach. His thigh slides in between my legs and I let out a sigh, but when my phone chirps, that sigh turns into a frustrated growl. I try to ignore it, wiggling my body against his, but when it chirps again I pull back. My eyes open, and I see it's nearly dark, the sun just barely visible over the horizon.

"Shit," I curse, pulling my phone from my back pocket. "What time is it?"

When I click my phone face on and see the time, I curse again knowing I really screwed up. We were supposed to be home in time for supper and that's in ten minutes. Meemaw and Peepaw have dinner every night at 6:00 p.m. on the dot, and if I miss, after I agreed to be there, they might not trust me anymore.

I pull the message up and see a short text from Meemaw.
Dinner's almost ready.

"Shit, shit, shit. We gotta go," I tell him, worried. "Dinner is almost ready."

"Shit," he mimics me, pulling back and following my charge to the truck. "Don't worry, I can get us there."

He catches up, giving me a quick peck on the cheek as we race back. I didn't realize how far we'd walked and it takes us a good five minutes to get back even jogging. When we make it, even though we're running late, this amazing man still takes the time to open my door, and I can't help the flutters that burst from my chest.

As we ride back to the house, Blake speeding but still being careful, I don't think I've ever felt so happy. Sure we got interrupted, but honestly, it's probably better this way. I know I talk a big game, and I'm a Nymph and all, but really, I'm not sure how I would feel about our first time happening so quick or that it would be in the woods up against a tree. As hot as that sounds, I don't think I want that to be our *first* time. And just to be clear, Blake and I *will* have a first time.

FREAKING LEPRECHAUN

My schedule was weird this week, so I haven't seen Blake since we had dinner at Meemaw and Peepaw's on Tuesday. He hasn't even called, and I hate to admit how much that bothers me. It's not like we're in a committed relationship or that there's some sort of rule that if you kiss a girl you have to call her within twenty-four hours. Actually, there should be a rule like that. Regardless, I really thought he would.

But since he didn't, I spent the last four days worrying about why. Did I do something wrong? Did something happen at dinner that upset him? It could be anything. Although, as far as I was concerned, dinner went really well, and that kiss out by the lake, well, I think we all know how well that went. I haven't stopped thinking about it. Scratch that, I haven't stopped dreaming about it; daydreaming, night-dreaming, shower-dreaming. Yes, I said shower-dreaming. Just look away.

But now that it's Saturday and I'm about to go in for my shift, I'm not sure what to expect, and I'm freaking the hell out. What if he thinks it was a mistake, or worse, he decided to stick to his rule of no relationships for a year? How much longer would I have to wait? I mean, I only have ten months left before I need to be back in Fay, and I need to enjoy my *'me time'*. I wanted that time to be with Blake, but now I just don't know. I guess there's only one way to find out.

My heels crunch the gravel under my feet as I cross the parking lot to the front door of The Oasis. I expect Blake to open the door for me, but when my feet hit the concrete walkway and the door remains closed, my worries ramp up another notch. I open the door for myself, which is kind of bullshit, and step inside the dimly lit bar. Nothing seems out of the ordinary. That is, until my eyes land on the bar.

A man I've never met before stands behind the bar top, a drink in one hand, a cell phone in the other. He speaks animatedly to two guys seated on the other side of the bar, but from here I can't hear what he's saying. I'm frozen in my spot as I wonder where Peg is and who the hell this joker is. I don't know if I've mentioned this, but I do *not* like change. Unless I approve it, and *only* if I approve it. And I do *not* approve of whatever this is.

Something catches my eye and I turn, Blake's gorgeous form moving toward me. He gives me the tiniest of smiles before motioning me right back out the front door.

Oh, now I'm really freaking out.

"What's going on?" I whisper-hiss the question, the suspense killing me.

"I'm not really sure," he says, shoving each hand in the pockets of his faded blue jeans. "The story is, Peg is really sick and is gonna be in Dallas for a few weeks having some tests run."

My hand flies to my chest in shock. "Oh my gosh. Is she gonna be okay?"

He shrugs. "I don't know. The whole deal is weird. I've lived here my whole life and I've never met this man. I think he said his name is Jim. He says he's lived here for nearly ten years, and he and Peg are life-long friends. He said Peg asked him to run the bar while she's gone."

"Should we call Peg?"

"I did," he confirms with a nod. "She answered her phone on the first ring, and while she did sound a little off, it could be that she really is sick. She confirmed what this guy said, and then she said she'd check in next week before hanging up."

"Weird."

"Yeah, it's a whole lot of weird." His eyes flit around the area, paranoid. "I don't know. I just get a bad vibe from this Jim guy." He rocks back on his heels, eyeing me as he does. "Anyway, I just wanted to give you a heads-up. Plus, two of those guys from the other night are in there, and it's clear they are friends with Jim."

Shit. "You mean the ones you beat the holy hell out of." It isn't really a question, more an acknowledgment.

He snorts, making him even hotter in my eyes as he takes a step closer to me. "For the record, I'll beat the holy hell out of *anyone* that lays a hand on you."

Again I say, swoon.

But also, this asshole didn't call me, and I'm not the kind of fairy that lets something like that go. "Oh yeah? Well, I thought maybe you changed your mind since I hadn't heard from you."

He opens his mouth to speak but then closes it. He seems unsure of himself. "I didn't know what the protocol was. I didn't want to come off like a stalker or anything."

"Okay, well from now on, you call."

He salutes me before giving me a, "Ma'am, yes ma'am," and I totally forgive him. "I promise to call you every single day as long as you'll let me." His hand slips out of his pocket, rising up and cupping my chin. He leans down, placing a chaste kiss on the corner of my mouth before leaning back with a grin. "We should go. Don't wanna be late with the new boss and all."

I agree before allowing him to lead me back inside, the door slamming behind us. We part ways as he moves toward the far back and I head to the bar. This Jim guy turns, giving me a look as I approach. You know how you see someone for the first time, and you just immediately don't like them. Yeah, this is one of those times. I do *not* like his face.

Reaching for my tray and money caddy, I turn, and seeing two of the fairies from the other night, I roll my eyes. This is going to be a long ass night. I'm so not in the mood for any of this.

Stepping away from the bar, I'm stopped when Jim gives me a questioning look. "And you are?"

"Ell," I tell him. "You must be Jim. The *temporary* boss." I use temporary on purpose, and from the look on his face, it irritated him.

I don't wait for him to respond, instead turning to wait on my tables. It's already pretty crowded and I don't see Liz, which means she probably called in sick. I'll have to thank her for that later. That was sarcasm in case you missed it.

I take a few orders, wishing I could do my job while avoiding Jim, but it's not possible with him tending the bar. I don't know what it is, but something about him gives me the heebie-jeebies. I'm no aura expert, but his is really strong *and* dark.

After I make a full round, I slip toward the back and decide to chat with Blake for a few minutes. I keep an eye on my tables, just in case, as he turns on his stool to face me.

"I don't like this guy," I confess. "I don't know what it is, but I don't like him, at all."

His hand sneaks out, his finger slipping through my belt loop as he tugs me a little closer. "Yeah, me too."

I can't even pay attention with him this close. All I want is for everyone else to disappear and for Blake to slam me up against the wall. Yes, I realize that was graphic. My mind is a dark and dirty place.

Blake spins me, my back now pressed to his knees. His hand continues to toy with my side as his other hand slides up my back. From my position, I can enjoy everything he's doing, but no one else can see. Plus, I can still keep an eye on the customers and the...

Shit.

I jerk forward, Blake's hands dropping from my body as I move to get a better look. I try to convince myself I'm wrong; that there's no way this is possible, but I know what I saw so it's just not working. I take a few steps forward, hearing Blake quietly say my name, but I ignore him. I turn my head sideways, trying to get the light just right, and as Jim's face finally comes into view, all my doubt washes away.

Jim is a Leprechaun.

***

Fuck my life.

My boss is a freaking Leprechaun. Not only do Leprechauns suck on a good day, but there is no reason for Jim, a Leprechaun, to be here. Not to mention it pretty much confirms our worries about Peg. You'll never make me believe Peg keeps that kind of company. Never. Peg is one-hundred percent human, and while obviously I'm a fairy and around her, I'm also awesome, and Leprechauns are not.

I call them *cons* for a reason. They'll legit con you out of your house, car, clothes, whatever. They'll take it all and you won't even realize what's happening. They're also freaking hoarders. Have you ever been to a Leprechaun's house? Yeah, don't. Trust me. I've seen the show, and they belong on it.

On top of their con ways and their hoarding tendencies, they're also more likely to be gifted with the mark of the Devil. There are almost as many UnSeelie Leprechauns as there are UnSeelie Elves. And while UnSeelie Elves are evil and manipulative, in my opinion, they don't hold a candle to these creepy little red-headed bastards.

Now, moving on.

Why in the actual hell is a *con* here in The Oasis pretending to be Peg's lifelong friend? It makes me wonder if she's even really sick. I mean, I know Blake said he talked to her, but now that I know Jim is a fairy, it's possible that conversation was influenced by magic. So, does that mean she's okay and Jim made her say that? Or has he done something bad to her? And if that's the case, why? I mean, I know I haven't been here long, but nothing up to this point would lead me to believe Peg knows about Fay or the existence of fairies. I'm not all knowing, but I just don't get that vibe from her. Plus, The Oasis is a hole-in-the-wall. Don't get me wrong, I love it here, but there's no way the bar is making enough money to attract a *con*.

That realization has me worried this has something to do with me. This is no longer about coincidence. This *has* to be about me, and while that's more than a little worrisome, I'm freaking out more for Peg, and I will get to the bottom of this.

Right. Now.

I'm standing just this side of the bar, staring dead on at the man in question as he shakes a drink-shaker. His glamour is good. Really good. I didn't even notice what he was the first half of the night, but now that *my* magic broke *his*, I can see it all. His red hair is cropped short on the sides and back, while remaining long and curly on the top. The armpits of his shirt are stained yellow causing me to shiver as I lower my gaze. He has a pot belly that hangs loosely over the brown belt that barely holds up his brown trousers, and while I can't see his shoes from here, I have no doubt they'll be loafers with a gold tassel. Cons love that shit. Such weirdos.

Jim catches me staring, nodding in my direction and asking, "What ya need?"

I hold two fingers up before mouthing, "Bud Light." Hopefully I can actually sell those, but if not, it's worth it. I need him to come closer. Even though I know I'll find the UnSeelie mark on the inside of his wrist, I need to see it with my own eyes. I need to know for sure.

Jim finishes mixing a drink before pouring it in a short glass and sliding it across the bar to one of the other fairies. I notice there's no money exchanged which surprises me. We don't do tabs here, but I guess it's possible Jim might not have that rule. Or, he's giving his shit-head friends free drinks at Peg's expense.

A growl bubbles up in my throat as Jim reaches down and retrieves two Bud Lights from the cooler under the counter. He walks them down to me, setting them on my tray as it rests on the bar top. As he pulls his wrist away with a nod, I see it. Right there, a fucking UnSeelie mark. Flaming wings. They'd actually be beautiful if I didn't know what they symbolize. His magic makes the flames appear to flicker, and for half-a-second I wish mine did that. Mine just glow. I shake that off, grabbing my tray and stomping off, trying to figure out what to do.

Halfway back to Blake I'm stopped by an older gentleman. "Those for sale, sweetie?"

"Yes, sir," I confirm, handing them off and taking his money quickly.

I leave him, avoiding the hand waving two tables over and slide in next to Blake. I'm not sure what to say though. It's not like I can say, "*Hey, Jim is a Leprechaun.*" Yeah, I'm sure that would go over really well.

Blake bumps me with his shoulder, pulling me back from la-la land. "What's up?"

I let out a ragged sigh, turning my gaze to his. "I don't know. I think we need to call Peg again or something. I just can't shake this feeling that something is not right; that something bad has happened to Peg. And where's Liz?"

"She called in sick yesterday and today."

My eyes widen in surprise. I talked to Liz yesterday. She didn't sound sick to me. "Who worked then?"

"Hannah."

"Okay, well, I wanna call Peg and now I wanna check on Liz." He gives me a questioning look. "I'm serious, I have a bad feeling, Blake. I can't stress that enough."

"Me too. I can't decide if I'm just being paranoid or if Jim is a serial killer."

"Agreed."

He pulls me to him, wrapping his arm around my middle before tilting my chin up so our eyes meet. "Okay, I'll come get you tomorrow morning. We'll run by Liz's first, and then Peg's. If Peg isn't home, we'll call her. Okay?"

I nod, leaning my head in to rest on his inviting shoulder. "Thank you."

BEE STINGS

I stressed all night last night about Liz and Peg. All I could think about was what if Jim has done something bad to both of them? What if their absences are related? It could be a coincidence but it seems awfully convenient to me. The good news is, we're about to find out. Blake promised me we would check on Liz and Peg first thing this morning, and now we're almost to Liz's house.

    We round the last corner at a snail's pace and I spot Liz's car parked in the driveway. That makes me feel a little better, although I'm not sure why. It's not like it's a guarantee if Jim took Liz he took her car too. I'm so dumb.

    I shake my head at my own ignorance and Blake notices. He gives me a questioning look but I just wave him off as he pulls to a stop and I get out. He pauses at the front of the truck, a disappointed look on his face and I realize he was coming to open my door for me. This man, y'all. How did I get this lucky?

    I stop in front of him, stretching up on my tiptoes and even then he has to lean down a bit so I can reach. "I'm sorry. I'm just anxious to make sure Liz is okay." I place a soft kiss on his perfect lips before pulling back with what I hope is a sincere look.

    "It's okay. I understand." He runs his hand down my cheek before resting his forehead against mine.

    Slipping his hand in mine, he leads me up the sidewalk to the front door where he knocks twice softly. Ugh, no one is going to hear that. I push him aside, pounding my fist against the metal screen door at least five times. I hear someone yell from inside, but I can't make out who it is, and when they don't open the door right away, I bang two more times.

"Hold your horses, damn. I'm comin'."

I immediately let out a sigh of relief at hearing Liz's exasperated tone, and when she swings the door open wide, her hand fixed to her hip, I feel even better.

"What the hell?" she demands, her hip cocked.

"Sorry, we were just worried," I tell her, throwing my arms around her neck and squeezing.

She's hesitant in returning my affection, as if she doesn't understand why, and I'm sure she doesn't. She pats my back lightly in the universal sign for, *dude, get off me*, and I step back slightly.

"What's up with her?" she asks Blake, pointing her thumb in my direction.

He pushes past Liz, not waiting to be invited in. "It's a long story."

Now she gives *me* a questioning look, but with a shrug I follow my man's entrance. We end up in the living room, Blake and I on the loveseat where we first got to know each other, and Liz sitting in a horrid, floral high-back chair.

Liz taps her foot impatiently, and when Blake and I neither one offers an explanation, she demands one. "Somebody better get to talkin'. Why are y'all beating on my door at 8:00 a.m. on a Sunday?"

I take in a deep breath. "You've been missing for two days, Peg is missing, and we have a new boss and he's a Le…" I stop myself just short of really fucking shit up. "He's a lame ass." Okay well, that was a stupid cover up. Lame ass? You couldn't come up with something better than that? And from the looks of it, Liz is thinking the same thing. I don't even want to look at Blake right now.

"*Okay*," Liz draws out. "But I'm not missing. I just needed a couple days to myself, so I called in sick. I figured you and Hannah could use the extra cash anyway. No harm, no foul."

"Well, we know that now," I whine. "But we thought you were dead."

Blake clears his throat. "*We* did not think you were dead. She did." He throws a thumb in my direction, and I give him a death glare deciding he and I need to have a talk about having each other's backs if we're going to make this relationship work. Really, he just needs to remember that I'm always right. End of story.

"Fine, *I* thought you were dead then." I throw one more evil look in Blake's direction and he throws his hands up in surrender.

"Whatever," Liz shrugs. "Why exactly did *you* think I was dead?"

Before I can answer, Blake cuts me off. "*We* both get a creepy vibe from this Jim guy."

"Oh, it's *we* now," I butt in, my head bobbing and weaving.

He reaches over, wrapping my hand in his as he nods. "Yes."

I'm melting.

Liz waves her hands, gesturing to Blake and I. "Can you two stop, *whatever* this is, and explain to me why you thought a creepy feeling about this Jim guy meant I and Peg were dead somehow?"

I give my man a coy smile. "I'll take this one, *sweetie*." He returns my smile, so I turn back to Liz.

I explain Jim's backstory, that Peg may or may not be sick, and that Blake talked to her. She doesn't seem to be as freaked out as I am, but she also hasn't met Jim. I have no doubt when she meets him, she'll have a different attitude.

When I'm done, Liz tucks her feet underneath her as she seems to think through everything I've said. "So, I take it you guys are going to Peg's next?"

"Yes," I confirm with a bob of my head.

"The whole story seems odd, so I definitely think we should check it out. I'm not on the schedule until Thursday, but if you need me to go up there before then just let me know."

I give her a smile and nod as Blake says, "I think we should head that way. Peg lives way out in the country."

He stands, pulling me to my feet before leading me to the front door. Liz follows behind us, and as we step out on the front steps, I turn back to her. "Let's stay in touch, okay? I know I've said this a dozen times, but I have a really bad feeling."

She pulls me in for a hug. "Okay. I'll text you non-stop if you want."

"I want."

We both laugh as I pull away, following Blake back to the truck.

***

The drive to Peg's took nearly thirty minutes, and when we started getting close, Blake decided to pull over and we walked the rest of the way. We cut through Blake's cousin's property, had to wade through a boggy area, and came up on the backside of Peg's land. Her house was on the opposite side, but Blake said this way we could get a look before anyone knew we were here. This is why he makes the big bucks, because I would have rolled up guns blazing.

It's a good thing we didn't too. As we crested the hill overlooking Peg's house, a car neither of us recognized was parked in the driveway. Blake had pulled me down to a crouch, and we'd crab-walked as close as he was comfortable with.

Now, we lie on our bellies near a set of bushes a few feet from the backdoor, the only sound, mine and Blake's labored breathing. Something crashes inside the house, and while I jump, I also try to climb over Blake. I know it should be the opposite, but I have magic. He does not. He gives me a confused look as he pulls me down, draping his arm over me as it should be.

He leans in close, his breath tickling my ear. "I want you to stay here. I'm going to get a closer look."

I open my mouth to stop him but it's too late, he's already moving, and I have no choice but to knock him out, with magic that is. I wiggle my fingers, because I'm one for the dramatics, as I wish for him to sleep. I top it off with a little extra, allowing the magic to lower him softly to the ground, his body cushioned in a bed of lush, green grass; wouldn't want to damage the goods. I'm gonna need those later.

I eye him quickly, and then realize I'll need to cover up my magic stream, but I don't have time for that right now. I need to figure out what that crash was, and who the hell is inside. Crawling to the window near the back door, I slowly raise up to take a peek. There are thick, blue curtains in my way, but I figure since I already had to use magic, I might as well go all out. I pull from my magic well, and with a flutter, the curtains move an inch, allowing me a perfect line of sight into the living room but not so much that it would be obvious. It's dark inside, which is odd, but I can just make out the shadowy figures of what I think are four men. Three sit on the couch, another sits straight-backed in a lounge chair. No sign of Peg anywhere. I've used a lot of magic already, and it's going to make me super sick to clean it up, but I need to know who's in there.

Needing to make sure I have all the details before I make any decisions, I move to do a quick perimeter check first. I crawl on my hands and knees through the weeds, checking in every window I can reach. On the far side, I come to a window that reveals what I'm pretty sure is Peg's bedroom. The bed is made, and nothing seems out of place, but as I move to magic the curtains back in place, something catches my eye. I press my face to the window, straining to see. A silver picture frame lies in the middle of the floor between the bed and the dresser. The glass is shattered, but I can't make out who's in the picture itself. Oh well, it doesn't really matter anyway.

With a sigh, I file that away for later, and repositioning the curtains with a flick of my wrist, I make my way back to the back window. I check first to make sure Blake is okay, and when it's clear he's sleeping like a log, I head over to the window before peering inside with a little magic. The men are all in the same position, and they appear to be talking. The one in the chair flings his hand back and forth, and I can see his mouth moving. The other three bob their heads enthusiastically, as if totally engrossed in what the other is saying. *I need to know* what he's saying. What could one more little magic hurt? I've already used way too much as it is, so what does it matter at this point?

My stomach does a flip as I release enough magic to be able to eavesdrop on the men's conversation, this one requiring much more from me. Within seconds, their voices come in loud and clear, one of them immediately recognizable. *Jim*.

My nose scrunches up in disgust at the sound of his voice, and it's all I can do to keep from charging in there and demanding he tell me where Peg is. Even if we're wrong about the Peg situation, I'm not wrong about Jim being an UnSeelie Leprechaun, which means he's up to something. He has to be. There is no good reason for a Leprechaun to be in Electra, Texas.

"We'll need to keep an eye on that security guard," Jim says, irritation in his tone. "And the girl too. The waitress. There's something off about that girl. I just can't put my finger on it, and we can't afford any mishaps when we're this close."

"Nothing off about her, boss. She's fucking hot as hell," one of the other fairies adds with a whistle.

I'd bet my left tit that's the one that slapped my ass the other night. A-hole.

"Yes well, be that as it may, your job isn't to fuck the help," Jim says calmly. "Jasper, you keep an eye on her since Melvin can't be trusted. And then Melvin and Borin, you two keep an eye on the guard."

Melvin? Ew.

"Understand?" Jim barks, losing his cool for the first time.

"Got it, boss," they say in unison, sounding like drones. That surprises me. It isn't often a Leprechaun gives orders to an Elf, or in this case, Elves; plural. Typically, it's the other way around. That makes this whole situation even more suspect.

I watch as the three fairies leave their seats before crossing to the front door. I hear the door shut with a thud, and then a car out front starts. I leave my place, letting the magic go so I can crawl back to Blake's side. He lightly snores and I smile, having to suppress a giggle. Heavy footsteps sound behind me and I whip around, assuming Jim is right behind me, but when I turn, no one is there. It must have come from inside, but the longer we stay here, the more likely we are to get caught.

I sprinkle a little magic on Blake's face, not waking him but making him feather light. I crouch-walk away from the house, pulling Blake behind me with a light grip on his shirt. We make it to a small grouping of trees and I stop, deciding to wake him up now. The problem is, I need to figure out what I'm going to tell him. Not only do I have to come up with a reason he missed all the action, I also need to figure out how much to tell him about what I heard. Obviously, I didn't hear much. But I did hear enough to confirm our suspicions about Jim. If he wasn't doing something wrong, then why would he need his three goons to keep an eye on me and Blake? And to be clear, I know I'm the waitress he was talking about. There's zero doubt in my mind.

As far as Blake is concerned, I need to keep this vague. I have to say just enough to make sure he continues to think Jim is a sketchy dick, but not so much that he starts to suspect something is weird about me personally. It really would be easier if I just told him the truth, but the truth terrifies me. I know we haven't known each other long, but I can't imagine losing him, especially over this.

A bee buzzes near my hand and I allow the cute little thing to land. "Thanks, little guy. You just gave me an idea." He emits a *'buzz-buzz'* before flitting away.

Leaning over Blake's prone, hot-as-sin body, I hover my hand over his head. Just as I'm about to wake him though, a voice floats to me on the wind. "I feel you. I can *feel* your magic. You aren't very good at covering it up."

Shit. I forgot to clean up the magic stream. Stupid, stupid, stupid. I mentally hit my head as the voice returns.

"I don't know who you are or why you're here, but I'll give you a warning. Leave Electra and don't look back, because if I catch you out here again, I won't stop until I figure out who you are. And when I find you, you'll pray to the Devil I hadn't."

The wind dies down and with it his words. My body shakes with his threat, but I know I can't worry about that right now. I focus on my magic all around the property, floating this way and that, and I suck it back in. It caresses my skin, as if coming home, before seeping into every pore on my body. It fills me to the brim, my stomach turning sour as too much hits me at once. I don't know how much longer I can keep this up. In Fay, if I used magic, I wouldn't have to pull it back in. On Earth, I'm overflowing, and it's going to eventually catch up to me. Sooner rather than later, I'll have to figure out a way to get rid of some of it in a way that doesn't lead Jim or my dad straight to me, but right now, I need to get Blake the hell out of here.

With a quick twinkle, I wake him slowly, enjoying watching his eyes flutter open. He lets out a yawn followed by a small smile and then his eyes burst open as he sits up with a start.

"What's going on? What's happening?" He runs his hands all over my body as if he's searching for injury. When he doesn't find any, his confusion only increases.

"It's a long story, but there's no time. We need to get out of here, now."

His eyes widen in worry as he nods his head in understanding. We work our way slowly back over the hill and once we're past, we both feel comfortable standing upright and walking the rest of the way. Neither of us says a word on the way back to the truck. Not even when Blake opens the door for me and I hop in. When he gets in and starts the truck before pulling away though, I know the silence is about to end.

He drives a few miles down the road before pulling into a pasture and cutting the engine as he turns to me. "Talk. I don't remember anything. What the fuck is going on?"

I wince at his tone, and he reaches over, grabbing my hand. He gives it a squeeze as a form of apology and I suck in a breath trying to buy myself some time. I remember my little bee friend, and having nothing better to say, I have no choice but to lie and I really hate doing that. Sure I've been lying by omission the whole time I've known him, but that's different. Okay, I know it's not, but back off.

With another breath, I consider magic'ing this situation away, but I know that would only be postponing the inevitable. "Are you allergic to bees?"

His head jerks back at my seemingly odd question. "What? Bees?"

"Yes, bees. Are you allergic?" Now I'm just annoyed. Just let me lie already.

"I mean, yeah. Why?" His head cocks to the right in confusion as he waits for me to elaborate.

"You got stung and then you just passed out. It was the craziest thing." I open my mouth to continue, but shut it quickly. The best lie is a vague lie. Do *not* elaborate.

"Weird," he says, scratching his head. "Where at?"

"Outside the house," I explain like it should be obvious.

He shakes his head with a smirk. "You're adorable, you know that?" He raises my hand to his lips, leaving a kiss there before adding, "I meant, where was I stung?"

Shit. "Uh, your head, I think."

He pulls his hand from mine, running it through his hair looking for the bee sting he won't find. Also, can we just address how lucky I just got that he is, in fact, allergic to bees? Almost too convenient, right?

When he doesn't find any painful spots, he drops his hand with a sigh before starting the truck. "I'm glad nothing bad happened while I was out. Did I miss anything important?"

Oh yeah, you missed a lot.

NINJA-SPY-SNOOP-FEST

It's been four days since our little recon mission, and there's been no word from Peg. We've all tried calling her, and while Blake talked to her when all this started, none of us have been able to reach her since. After we left her house Sunday, I had to make up some bullshit to tell Blake since it's not like I can just outright tell him Jim is a freaking Leprechaun. I told him I overheard him saying some shady shit about me, and that he insinuated Peg wasn't sick at all. None of that is really true, and I hated lying, but what other choice did I have?

Oddly, Blake had bought my tall-tale without question, which only made me feel worse. I've seen him every day this week, and every time I get closer and closer to telling him who and what I really am, but each time something stops me. I pay close attention to the universe. I mean, it led me to Blake, so I figure if it wanted me to spill-the-beans to him right now, I wouldn't even hesitate.

As it is, I can't stand to think about how he'll react. He could legit hate me. Maybe just because I lied. But maybe, and I know I've said this before, but humans fear what they don't understand. What if he hates me solely because I'm different? I just don't know that I could live with myself if he hated me. I'm really falling for this man, and every day that passes we grow closer and closer. I know it's all going to end eventually. Obviously I have to go home at some point, and when I do, I'll either have to tell him or leave him behind. Neither option sounds appealing.

Whether I tell him or not is irrelevant right now, because I care about him enough at this point that I feel the need to protect him. I know he'd say that's his job, but he doesn't know what I'm capable of. Hell, I'm not even sure what I'm capable of. I just know that Peg is missing, there's a Leprechaun in town, and I somehow feel it's related to me. But why? What on God's green Earth could an UnSeelie want with me?

I have no idea, but I have every intention of finding out. The best way to do that; snooping. It might be my day off, but I'm heading in for a little, old-fashioned ninja-spy-snoop-fest. Luckily, Blake is off work tonight too. I don't want him anywhere near this, and that's exactly why I didn't tell him where I was going to be tonight. I think I hurt his feelings when we left lunch today. I told him I couldn't hang out tonight. It hurt my heart, but I'm sucking it up because it's worth it if he stays safe.

Peepaw let me borrow the truck since he and Meemaw had no plans tonight, and as I pull in the gravel parking lot of The Oasis, I smile, realizing I'm actually getting pretty good at driving 'ole Bessie. I choose an empty spot on the far side of the lot, and turning the engine off, I hop out and attempt being casual as I saunter to the front door. I have to open the door myself since Blake isn't here which sucks, but I guess I'll get over it. The door swings wide, dust particles visible in the ray of light slipping in the dimly lit bar. It takes my eyes a second to adjust, but when they do, I see Hannah is behind the bar and Jim is nowhere to be seen. With a quick scan, I don't see any of his friends either so I decide to check in with Hannah.

"Hey," she greets me as I plop down in the brown highback barstool.

"Hey, girl, hey." I order a drink, and while Hanna makes my cherry coke, I chat her up. "So, you the only one here tonight; no boss?"

She glances around cautiously before rolling her eyes. "If you mean Jim, yeah, he's here. He and his asshole cronies are in the office. Been back there about an hour. I mean, I know it's fucking Wednesday, but damn. He left me out here tending bar *and* waiting tables."

Well, I guess she's talkative today. "Yeah, that sucks. I'm

gonna stick around for a few if you need some help." Seeing the look of appreciation sweep across her face, I add, "Let me pee first."

She nods, setting my ready drink down behind the bar and I leave, headed down the back hall. The first two doors are the men's and women's bathroom, but that's not where I'm actually headed. I pass both doors and coming to a third, I slow. The door to Peg's office is shut, but with a little magic I'm able to listen right in. I know I said I shouldn't be using magic unless I want to get caught, but I can't just ignore the fact that Peg is most likely hurt. Or, she will be if I don't do something.

The first thing I hear through the door is a voice I don't recognize. "Yeah well, fuck the King."

My hand flies to my mouth, covering up my near gasp. King Rowan, my uncle, is fairly well liked. You rarely hear anyone speak of him in a poor light. Even the UnSeelie have settled somewhat since he's been king. There hasn't been a single war between the Seelie and Unseelie since he was crowned, and that's saying a lot. Before that, Fay was in a perpetual state of war.

The room goes quiet for more than a few seconds, and I worry I'm about to get caught, but then I hear Jim's voice. "Be patient. We won't have to worry about him much longer. One of the strongest sources of energy lies underneath this little shithole town, and once we have everything we need, Electra will be ground zero. It's only a matter of time."

What the hell are they planning? I mean, I knew Electra was a source of great energy, but what do they intend to do with it?

Jim's devious laugh assaults my ears and I tone my magic down a bit. "Once the King is dead, we'll have everything we could ever want."

Fuck.

***

Hannah is probably pissed at me. After hearing Jim say the King would soon be dead, and realizing they were plotting something horrible, I'd rushed out of the bar without looking back. I'd even forgotten to clean my magic up, but right now that's the least of my worries.

I was on the schedule to work last night, but I called in sick. It hadn't even been a total lie. All the magic use while on Earth has left me with some nasty magic sickness, so that on top of everything else, I just couldn't make myself go. I hadn't even answered my phone when Blake called me a dozen times, and when he'd shown up this morning and gave Meemaw flowers for me, I felt like a real bitch. Bitch or not, I just can't face him right now. There's no doubt in my mind he's about to find out I'm a fairy, either because I tell him or because this bullshit blows up and he figures it out on his own. It'll most likely be because this place is about to be crawling with Seelie guard. There's no way I can get away with not telling my dad. And when I do, he'll come in with the full force of Fay behind him. The bad part is they'll magic everyone's memories away when they're done and Blake won't even know who I am. That breaks my heart more than anything.

That's really why I'm lying in bed at four p.m. knowing I'm supposed to be at work in an hour. My little fairy-tale in Electra is about to come crashing down, and there isn't a damn thing I can do to stop it. Trust me, I've tried to think of something, anything. But no matter how hard I try to imagine a different outcome, it always ends the same.

My thoughts switch to Blake. He really is an amazing man. Despite his gruff outward appearance, he's kind and thoughtful, a real gentleman, and it surprises me more than I can say at how lucky I got meeting him. I feel genuinely cared for when I'm around him, and I don't want to lose that. I wanna keep him, damn it. But I just don't know how that's possible. Even if he takes the news of me being a fairy well, and even if my dad was to let me bring him to Fay, humans don't do well in my realm. It's just too much energy for them. There are some humans who live in Fay though, so maybe I could find them and figure out how they manage to live without issues.

I clutch my pillow tighter, because I just know that's not going to happen. I need to let Blake go now before this gets any worse for him or me. The closer we get, and the more time we spend together, the harder this is going to be.

With a grunt, I drag myself from bed. As much as I want to call in, I can't. It's Friday night. Liz would kill me. And while she won't know me either in just a few days, I really love that girl and want to enjoy the last little bit of time I have with her.

I grab a pair of black jeans off the floor because, who cares, and tug them on, bouncing around the room and nearly busting my ass. Searching through my bag, I find a bright-red halter-top and decide, why not? I give my hair a quick brush through but don't bother fixing it, and slap on a thin line of red lipstick before grabbing my shoes and leaving the room.

Halfway out the bedroom door, I pause, my hand sliding over my back pocket. Realizing I forgot my phone, I turn back and rush to the bedside table before grabbing it and slipping it into its place. Leaving my room again, I cross the living room headed for the kitchen. Meemaw stands over the stove, an adorable apron secured around her waist, and whatever she's cooking smells amazing. I'm starting to associate the smell of her cooking with home, and my heart twists at the thought. She turns over her shoulder giving me a smile, and my eyes well up with tears. Soon, I won't ever see that smile again. My dad will never let me out of his sight once I go back and tell him what's going on here. And even if he would let me bring Meemaw and Peepaw with me, I can't expect them to uproot their lives for little 'ole me. Plus, I'd be in the same situation as I am with Blake, humans and Fay don't mix.

Meemaw misinterprets my tears and sets the ladle down before rushing to me, wrapping me up in a wonderful, warm hug. "Oh honey, you're still sick. Just call in. Peg will understand."

Peg isn't there.

I shake my head, but she shushes me. "Honey, if this is about money, you don't need to worry about that. You don't owe us anything."

I sniffle. "It isn't. I'm fine; promise."

Pursing her lips, she places her hands on her hips in a defiant stance. "No, I won't hear of it. You're staying home. I'll call Peg myself."

I open my mouth to argue, but a knock at the front door stops me. I hear John shuffle across the living room as I ask Meemaw, "Are you expecting anyone?"

She shakes her head, and I don't know why, but the universe is giving me a really bad feeling. I rush past Meemaw, storming out of the kitchen. When the front door comes into view, I'm stopped in my tracks. I don't know if this is bad, but at least it's not as bad as I thought. I imagined a full UnSeelie army at the front door, but thank God, it's just Blake.

"You have a gentleman caller," Peepaw shouts, not realizing I'm right behind him.

"I'm here," I answer, giving him a start.

He backs away from the door, giving me room to slip outside and on the porch with Blake. The door shuts, and I find myself nervous. My stomach is in knots as I debate telling Blake the truth now. Better for him to hear it from me than someone else, right?

"Feeling better?" Blake reaches for a strand of hair that's slipped past my shoulder and I flinch. I didn't mean to, but it's out there now, and the look on Blake's face is a crushed one. "What's going on, Ell?"

"Nothing, but what are you doing here?"

Now it's his turn to flinch, and I know I'm being too harsh, but it's just one of those things. You know what I'm saying. You wake up in a bad mood and it's impossible to change it until you go back to sleep and try again. Plus, I'm supposed to be pushing him away.

He takes a step back, crossing his arms tightly against his chest. "I tried to call you. Oasis is closed tonight. I didn't want you to drive in for nothing." He takes another step back, and I realize he's working his way to the steps. "Anyway, I'll let you get some rest, I guess."

"Wait." I don't leave my spot, keeping the space between us because if he touches me again, I won't be able to let him go. "Why is it closed?"

He shrugs, refusing to make eye contact with me. "Don't know. I went in and Jim said he wasn't opening tonight. Said he had some shit to take care of in Dallas."

"Do you think it has to do with Peg?"

"I don't know, Ell. The whole deal is weird, but I know I could use a night off, so I'm not gonna complain too much." He takes a few more steps closer to his truck before turning back to me. "I'm gonna go."

"Where are you going?" I shouldn't have asked that. I know. I'm supposed to be letting him go. But I just couldn't keep my stupid mouth shut. It's like I'm trying to make this harder on both of us.

"I guess I'll hang at the house." He walks backward, making it to the front of the truck before giving me his back.

I know I shouldn't care that he didn't ask me to join him, and I definitely deserve it, but God my heart hurts. It takes everything in me not to stop him as he climbs in his truck. My eyes fill with tears for the second time in the last few minutes, and I feel as if I can't get a breath. His truck starts, and for just a minute, he sits still as he stares straight ahead. For a second, I think he might get out, rush toward me, and snatch me up, refusing to walk away from me ever again. I know I shouldn't want that, but I do. Unfortunately, I'm not some chick in a rom-com, because all too soon, the engine revs and Blake pulls away, his truck disappearing in a plume of dust.

It's all I can do to stay upright. I want to collapse in a heap and ball my eyes out. No, what I really want is to rush after him, but I know I can't or I guess, shouldn't. A burning sensation fills my chest, and the realization that I love Blake hits me hard. I know I haven't known him for long, but I've said it all along, something drew me to him. I'm a fucking Nymph for shit's sake. I should've fucked dozens of guys by this point. But no matter how much I wanted to be a normal Nymph and sleep with every hot fairy in a thousand-mile radius, I just couldn't. Something has always told me I was waiting on something, or I guess, someone. There's no doubt in my mind now, that someone is Blake. That's going to make leaving him so much harder.

I mean, I guess if I told him and he took it well, he could come to Fay once I figure out a way to keep him from getting sick or dying from the energy, but even if I was successful, we could only ever be friends there. I'm expected to marry a Seelie, or a few Seelie if my dad has his way. You know, increase the odds of birthing a bunch of Seelie royals. So there's no way he'll let me have a human. It's rare for a human and a fairy to procreate, and even more rare for them to birth a Seelie-marked child.

I must have misunderstood the universe. There's no way Blake and I can be together, which means there's no way we're meant to be. I choke out a sob as I stumble forward. I can't stay here another second. Meemaw calls my name from inside, but I just can't face anyone right now. Checking to make sure my phone is in my back pocket, I take off, running away from the house without any clear destination.

Within minutes, I hit the tree line and don't look back. I use magic without a care as I slam branches and rocks against the trees around me, taking my rage out on the earth. A branch nearly slaps me in the face, probably as payback, but I manage to duck as I jump over a rotting log. I suck my magic back to me, welcoming the sickening feeling it causes in the pit of my stomach. Anything is better than the ache I feel knowing that was my last encounter with Blake.

I start to slow as I realize I'm getting close to the area where the veil is thin between the two realms; Fay and Earth. The portal is just the other side of the dirt road I now stand on as I try to will myself across. I need to go back. Right now. Not tomorrow. Now. I need to go back to Fay and tell my dad everything that's happened. He and my uncle need to know so they can stop whatever is coming. It would be better if I had all the information first, but I know there are smarter fairies than me back in Fay that can figure this out. Hell, for all I know they already know about the plot to kill the King. It's not like they share top-secret information with me. Not to mention I've been gone, so there's no telling what's been going on in my absence.

I force my legs to move, taking two steps on the dirt road, but stop when I hear a loud engine. I turn, a truck barreling toward me, and I barely manage to jump out of the way. I hear the tires fish-tail as I roll to a stop, the tiny rocks cutting my skin. My shoulder throbs as I try to sit upright, and when I hear my name, it sounds far away. I ache, and I'm pretty sure my shoulder is dislocated. I have zero tolerance for pain though, so it could just be a tiny bruise.

I hear my name again, but it sounds as if I have cotton in my ears. I close my eyes, just for a second, and the last thing I hear is, "Ell. Oh God, Ell."

THE MOMENT WE'VE ALL BEEN WAITING FOR

After my near death experience, I passed out. I'm not even sure why. Maybe it's the stress from the last few days. Or maybe it's just that I was nearly hit by a speeding truck. Seriously, my life flashed before my eyes and I was disappointed. All I could think was this is my worst nightmare; I'm gonna die a virgin.

But then, I heard the voice of a God. Or Blake, whatever. I couldn't understand why he was there, and he sounded so far away. With the direction he was headed, he could have only been going back to Meemaw and Peepaw's, but at the time, I was too woozy to think too hard about it. I remember his strong arms lifting me and placing me in the truck, but I'd been so sleepy. It was the oddest thing. When I woke, I was wrapped in a fuzzy black blanket, and a warm body was pressed to my back. The smell alone told me it was Blake, and I'd let out a sigh of relief. I mean, it really could have been the killer.

Now I've been lying here for over an hour, refusing to move an inch for fear I'll lose this feeling. I have never felt as safe and cared for as I do right now. My head rests on one of his arms, while his other drapes loosely over my middle. His chest rises and falls against my back, nearly lulling me back to sleep. I'd love nothing more than to roll over so I can watch him sleep. Yes, I know that's creepy. And, as much as I want to be a creeper, I don't want to risk waking him, so instead, I stay as still as I can. I'm terrified that the minute he wakes, everything will come crashing down. Nothing has changed. I still have to leave, and I still need to push him away. I need to make this easier, for him at least.

His throat clears behind me and I hold my breath. "I know you're awake, Ell." His words are a whisper in my ear, the movement of his breath tickling the side of my neck.

I guess the jig is up.

I roll over, casting my eyes up at his beautiful blue orbs as they fill with compassion. To look at Blake, you'd think he's a real hard-ass, but to know him, he's the exact opposite. He's kind and caring, loyal and loving; everything a fairy could want.

I guess he doesn't realize I'm quiet only because I'm mentally singing his praises, because he takes my silence harshly, pulling away from me causing a whine to slip past my throat. He stops his retreat, his hand on my hip the only part of us still touching.

"What's going on with you, Ell?"

I know I should just spill the tea, but when I open my mouth, I stumble around and can't bring myself to do it. With a sigh, I decide to go with a half-truth. "There are things about me and my past that you don't know, that I can't tell you."

His forehead scrunches in frustration. "There is nothing you could say that would make me love you less."

Both our eyes widen as what he just said hits us. My heart pounds in my chest so hard I'm certain he can hear it. He just inadvertently told me he loved me. And while my feelings for him are most definitely love, he hadn't said those words out loud yet. It's like a zing just zipped from his heart to mine, and I don't even care how corny that sounds.

As my love for him expands further, I have to know one more thing. "Why were you coming back?"

He tilts his head to the side. "What?"

"You were headed back to Meemaw and Peepaw's. Why?" I need to know. He may have just said he loves me, but that doesn't explain why he was coming back.

Before he can answer, his phone dings, a growl forced from the back of his throat. He attempts to ignore it, but when it dings again, he apologizes before rolling toward the nightstand on his side of the bed. I debate sneaking a peek over his shoulder, but I don't want to be that kind of girlfriend. Girlfriend. I just referred to myself as his girlfriend. Sigh. This just makes things so much harder.

When he rolls back over, an odd look is fixed to his features. "It's Jim. He's at the front door."

"Why?" I nearly choke on the question as he slips off the side of the bed.

"I don't know. His text said, *'I'm at the front door; need to talk'*." He shakes his head as he slips his boots on. "So weird."

"Yeah, weird."

Fuck. Fuck. Fuckity-fuck. This cannot be good. There is absolutely no good reason Jim would be here right now. They don't even know each other, really. It doesn't matter; whatever it is, I have zero qualms about killing that douche-canoe. Zero. I don't even care if I have to use magic in front of Blake. I'll do whatever it takes to keep him safe.

I roll from the bed, my bare feet hitting the cool hardwood floor. I don't bother with shoes; there's no time because Blake is already crossing the room. He makes it to the door and stops, my front hitting his back hard, and I let out an *'Oomph'* as he turns to steady me.

"Hey, you okay?" I bob my head as his hands slide up and down my arms. "Listen, something feels off about this. I need you to stay out of sight. I have no idea why, but when the universe speaks, you listen."

Oh my holy shit. Did he...did he just use my line? Well, there's no denying we were meant to be now. But that's just one more reason I need to keep him safe. How can I do that if I stay hidden? But, if I stay hidden, then I'll have the element of surprise when I use my magic to boil Jim's blood inside his veins. Yes, that was graphic. No, I don't know if that's possible.

Needing the element of surprise, I agree to stay hidden, and seeming satisfied, he turns and leaves me in the doorway. His breathing gets further away as I try to listen. I need to know the second Blake makes it to the front of the house. I agreed to stay hidden. I didn't agree to stay in the bedroom, so when I'm certain he's made it through the living room, I slink down the hall, using the wall to stay hidden. The front door creaks open, and I hear a few low words from Blake; most likely an irritated greeting. I consider using magic to hear better, but Jim knew I was at Peg's the other today because he sensed my magic, so I just can't risk it with him being this close.

"Have you seen Ell?"

Excuse me say what? Why the fuck is this fucker looking for me?

I strain to hear more, but Blake's words are too low. When I hear Jim answer, "Well, I need to speak to her. So if you see her, send her my way." Jim says something else, possibly a goodbye, and then the door closes with a thud. I slump against the wall, sinking to the floor with a sigh of relief. Well, that was close, and I didn't even have to boil his blood, at least for now.

***

"Ell, why are you in the floor?"

My eyes cast up to Blake as he looms over me and I shrug. "Ehh, seemed like a nice place to sit."

He doesn't seem convinced. "Uh-huh." He reaches down, grabbing me under the arms and lifts me to my feet. "So tell me, why would Jim be looking for you?"

Again I shrug, because honestly, I don't know. "I have no idea." And when he gives me a questioning look, I double down. "Seriously. I have no clue what he wants to see me about unless I'm about to get fired."

"Why would he fire you?"

I gurgle my spit in the back of my throat to prove my annoyance and I'm thrilled when Blake lets out a chuckle. He grabs my hand without another word and drags me toward the kitchen. Lifting me, he deposits me on the counter and goes about pulling things from the fridge.

"Um, so how did we go from the third degree to turkey sandwiches?" I watch as he spreads a thin layer of mayo on four slices of bread before layering on way too much turkey. "Unless those are both for you, easy on the turkey, buddy."

He snorts a laugh, removing a couple slices from one of the sandwiches before adding a thin, perfectly ripe slice of tomato. He doesn't answer my original question as he finishes up each sandwich with a few round pickles. When he's done, he hands one sandwich to me and takes a big bite out of the other before grabbing a couple beers from the fridge, setting them both on the counter next to me. I take a few bites of my sandwich, enjoying the normalcy of this moment, and when Blake moves to stand between my legs, giving me a look, I know our quiet moment is over. These damn turkey sandwiches were an evil ploy. That bastard. He knows food is the easiest way to get something out of me. It's a damn good thing he didn't offer me chocolate; I would have handed over my life story.

"In answer to your question," he starts, "I don't care."

The hurt must be evident on my face because he quickly pops the last corner of the sandwich in his mouth, swallowing quickly as he thumbs my chin. "That's not what I meant, Ell. I just meant, there's no point in giving you the third degree. If there's something going on, you'll tell me when you're ready. I meant what I said, I don't give a fuck about your past. I care about *you*, and nothing is going to change that."

I wouldn't be so sure.

His hand slips behind my neck as he eliminates the last bit of space between my legs. His other hand runs across my thigh quickly before landing on my ass. He squeezes, pulling me forward and I swallow the moan that nearly slips out.

"I don't know what's going on. I'm worried about Peg, sure, but if that mother-fucker even so much as smells you, I'll fucking kill him."

Purr. Down girl.

I always knew I was crazy, but I feel even more so at the realization that his threat of violence has me more turned on than I've ever been. My whole body hums, and I wish he'd just kiss me already. Maybe a little more than a kiss. Just a little.

I try to act nonchalant as I pop the last bite of my sandwich in my mouth, swallowing hard when his hand slides down my thigh. I wish these fucking jeans were gone. Why do I insist on wearing so many clothes?

"I love you, Ell. I know that seems crazy because we just met but it's true. I've never felt this way about anyone else, and if you were trying to push me away back at John's, well I'm sorry, I just can't let you do that."

Can someone please explain why he's still talking? I mean come on, he had me at the turkey sandwich for fuck's sake.

I absentmindedly...nope, that's a lie. I'm very, very cognizant of the fact that I just rubbed my V against his P. I just need him to help me out a little. I'm in. What doesn't he get about that? I'm all in. I don't care that I'm a fairy and he's a human and my dad might never let me see him again. *Carpe diem*. I'm about to seize this dick.

Damn, girl. That was lude.

I glance up, giving him my best doe eyes and he chuckles, sending shivers up and down my spine. But when he doesn't give me what I want, I let out a frustrated growl. At this point, I'll say and do anything he wants to get what *I* want.

I let out a whiney sigh, fisting his shirt in one hand and the hair at the base of his neck in the other. "I don't know what I gotta do to get you to kiss me, but damn. I love you. Yes. I. Love. You. Big facts. Okay?"

A sly grin peeks out from the corner of his lips, and then he's kissing me. This isn't like the first time we kissed. No. This time he isn't slow and tentative. This time he demands entrance to my mouth, our tongues dueling for dominance. Goosebumps break out across my arms and down the back of my neck as his hand grips my thigh tightly. His tongue is practically fucking my mouth and I moan, causing a growl to vibrate from his mouth to mine. He roughly grips me under each thigh, and I don't hesitate to latch my legs around his middle as he pulls me from my perch. His mouth never leaves mine as he carries me through the house, kicking the bedroom door wide to allow us entrance. I tug his hair, and he stops, too turned on to make it to the bed. He slams me against the wall, my back hitting hard. That's definitely going to leave a bruise, and I don't even care.

This is it folks, the moment we've all been waiting for.

I'm wedged between Blake and the wall as he fumbles with the string holding my top in place. I giggle at his frustration. I don't know why. Sometimes I giggle when I'm nervous. But also, this got real serious, real fast, and as much as I want to get fucked, this is also our first time together and I really want it to be something I remember for the rest of my life. Not just some random fuck, but the real deal. You only get one first time.

He pulls back, slowing for the first time, and seeing something in my eyes, he returns my giggle with a laugh of his own. He presses his forehead to mine and I stroke my fingers through his hair. A contented sigh leaves his mouth, and I cover it up with my lips. Our kisses are much slower now; almost languid. He carries me to the bed and throws the covers back, laying me down. It hits me suddenly that this is my first time but it most definitely isn't Blake's. What if I'm not good at this? What if he's disappointed?

His hand grips the back of his shirt prepared to pull it off, but my fear must be written on my face because he stops mid-motion. "What's wrong? We...don't have to do this. It just seemed like you wanted to. But if you don't, that's okay. I don't want you to feel like you have to just because I professed my undying love for you."

His joke relieves some of the nerves coursing through my body, and I hesitate telling him what has me slowing down, but I know I should. "I...this..." My finger points from me, to him, and back again as I struggle to find the right words.

When I don't get the words out right away, he says, "Seriously, it's fine, Ell. I promise."

"No," I practically shout as he lets go of his shirt. "It isn't that. I just, well, I haven't ever done this before."

His eyes widen in surprise as he lets out an, "Oh."

I'm worried for a half-a-second that he might not want me now, but when he climbs in bed and pulls me close, all that worry dissipates. He presses his lips to mine softly, my body melting against his. When he pulls back, he runs his fingers along my cheek before tucking a strand of my hair behind one ear.

He brushes his nose against mine, the act sending a shiver down my body. "I didn't realize. I'm glad you told me. Probably best if your first time isn't me fucking you up against a wall."

I laugh through my nose, causing him to laugh too as he swallows it up with a kiss.

"Are you disappointed?" I ask, nervous.

His head jerks back, eyes wide. "What? God no, Ell. Why would I be disappointed?"

"I don't know. I have no clue what I'm doing so I'll probably be horrible at it. If I don't do it right and you don't enjoy it…" My eyes cast down with that admission, embarrassed.

His hand grips my chin, forcing my eyes up. "There is *zero* chance I won't enjoy it. But if *you* aren't ready, it *is* okay. Just be honest."

My words are just a whisper, "I want to. I…Blake, I may have to leave soon and I don't know when I'll be back. I want to have this with you."

I can see the hurt in his eyes as he realizes the truth in my words; that I probably *won't* be coming back. Knowing that, *he* might decide he doesn't want to. It might not matter what I want.

A strand of my hair falls forward and he brushes it back carefully. "You'll come back."

Our lips meet and this time, I know we won't stop. I've never been kissed like this and yes, I know I've said that before, but this time I mean it. Each brush of his lips is filled with love as he reaches once more to pull off his shirt. I reach to do the same to mine but he stops me, our lips apart only by inches as he pulls my shirt over my head before chunking it across the room with a small smile. His hand drifts down my neck and across my chest as I lie there completely still. Each touch leaves behind dozens of goosebumps, and when he sneaks his hand around to my back and snaps my bra loose like a pro, I shiver. His lips sweep lightly across my jaw and down my neck, while his hand tentatively moves up and skims softly across my breast. Every inch of my body aches for him as his lips clamp around my nipple, sucking it in and then releasing it with a pop. I gasp at the sensation, his hair tickling my neck as he reaches to undo my jeans. When his mouth leaves me, I want to whine, but I hold it in at seeing the sight of him climbing down to remove my jeans. He carefully slips them off before doing the same to his, and then he presses his body against mine, holding most of his weight on his forearms. The skin-to-skin connection feels amazing; unlike anything I've ever felt before. His mouth returns to my breast, leaving licks and kisses as he goes, and a quiver starts at my scalp, working its way down my whole body.

I realize my hands are clasped just below my chin and I suddenly feel like an idiot. Why do I never know what to do with my hands? I feel like a freaking T-rex. I gotta work on that. I should be touching him too, right?

Almost as if reading my mind and without looking up, with one hand he separates mine and guides them up to the headboard. He secures a bar in each of my hands, and then he works his way back down; down, down, down.

When his fingers glide over my thin, plum colored panties, I can't help the moan that bubbles out. My eyes roll back in my head as he rubs back and forth just right. I'll rub one out just like the next girl, but *you a damn lie* if you say it feels anything like this.

The pressure below my pelvis builds to an all-time high, and I know if he keeps this up, I'm going to come crashing down. My grip tightens on the headboard bars, my toes curling tight. Blake seems to realize where I'm headed, and in one swift move, my panties are gone, joining his underwear somewhere in the floor. I feel him against me and I shudder, his dick hard against my aching clit. When I feel him nudge my entrance, I clench. From the feel of him, he's big, and I have a tiny vagina, so this might not work. I'm spiraling as he circles the head of his dick around my opening.

Sensing my change in mood he slows, leaning down close and connecting our eyes. "I'll go slow. I would never hurt you."

And that's all it takes for me to be right back in. Or on, whatever.

His hand slides down, gripping his shaft and guiding it in place. When the tip lines up and I feel him push, I tense from the pain for only a moment and then it's nothing but pure bliss. There's no way my eyes could roll back any further as he slowly buries himself inside me. Once he's fully seated, he glides in and out twice, made easy by how ready I am for him, and the pressure builds to the heavens.

He caresses my cheek, and I look to him with what I'm sure is a dopey smile. "You okay?" he asks.

I bob my head like a damn moron and he grins, sliding his hand down to the back of my thigh before forcing my knee to bend. He rocks back, and when he slams home again, I lose it. My back arches, egging him on, and an embarrassing sort of noise frees from the back of my throat. He lets go of my knee, confident I know not to move it, and slips his hand in between us, his fingers finding my most sensitive part with ease.

His thumb presses against my clit, and when he slams in again, he lets out a moan that only serves to drive me wild. "God, Ell. You're so tight. So perfect."

The only word I can manage is, "Fuck."

He works in and out as his thumb circles faster, a sensation unlike anything I've ever felt coming over me. It's like I'm at the very top of a roller-coaster and I'm about to come crashing down. He grunts again, and I know he's close too. My hands leave the bars, gripping his forearms and pulling him in, encouraging him to go harder, faster.

He doesn't disappoint and within seconds, I let out a very unladylike scream ending with, "Blake, yes!"

And then at the same time, we explode. His seed fills me, and I feel it leaking out, sliding down my thighs and ass. He stays stock still for the better part of a minute as my pussy continues to contract around his dick. He shudders, and I can't help but smile, knowing I did that to him. When he slides out with a squelch and rolls over pulling me with him, we both close our eyes, letting out an identical sigh of content.

DEAD-MAN-WALKING

Last night was epic. I never, in all my years of big talk, had imagined anything like that. Blake was more than amazing. And I could be imagining it, but something clicked with us last night. Not as in, we mesh well, no, as in like something physical or universal clicked into place. I felt connected to him on an otherworldly level. It was strong enough that *he* even mentioned it. When a human feels something like that, it's a big deal. Even *I* have never felt anything like that before. It's almost as if his energy is now part of mine, like we're tied together on a cellular level. I know that sounds weird, but I don't know how else to explain it.

    I still felt it this morning when we woke up, Blake's arms wrapped tightly around me. I can't express how good it felt to stay wrapped up together all morning as we lazily watched some show about getting engaged to someone you don't even know. It was actually addicting, and before long we'd ended up six episodes in. Eventually, though, we'd had no choice but to leave our comfortable spot so he could take me home. The drive there sucked, if for no other reason than I knew as soon as I stepped foot out of his truck everything would change. But the worst part was the goodbye on Meemaw and Peepaw's front porch when he held me tight and we kissed for what might be the last time. I'd been so upset, I bypassed Meemaw and Peepaw both as they sat close on their loveseat, heading straight for the shower where I balled my eyes out for at least an hour. Meemaw had come knocking twice, but I'd just told her I needed to be alone, which only made me feel worse; guiltier. I'd stayed in there so long, the water had turned a frigid temperature but I didn't even care.

When I'd gotten out of the shower, I dressed in jeans and a ratty t-shirt, and went searching for something to eat. Meemaw had left me a note on the counter that said they'd run to town to buy groceries but that she'd left me some leftover spaghetti in the fridge. Just another example of why I love that woman.

Now as I sit on the couch, enjoying the shit out of my noodles and homemade sauce, I know I can't keep putting off the inevitable, no matter how much I love it here. Every second I wait, I'm risking something bad happening to my uncle, maybe even my dad, or worse, my little sister. Not to mention the fact that I'm pretty sure that ass banana Jim knows who I am. There's no other reason I can think of as to why he would have needed to see me yesterday. Either he knows exactly who I am or, at the very least, he knows I'm the fairy that was sneaking around Peg's the other day. On top of that, either of those options puts my friends in danger; Liz, Blake, even Meemaw and Peepaw. I just can't risk that. These people are too important to me.

Swirling the last bite of noodles around my fork, I leave my comfy seat and make my way to the kitchen, depositing the bowl in the sink after giving it a good rinse. I trudge to my room, fully recognizing I'm stalling, and grab my bag from the closet floor. I'm already mostly packed, but I grab a few more things from around the room before zipping the bag closed. I take one more glance around, unable to stop the tears from falling, and then switching off the lights, I leave.

I hadn't planned to leave a note, but the more I think about it, the more that seems like a real shit thing to do. If I just disappear, I know Meemaw and Peepaw will be worried sick. It doesn't seem right to do that to them, especially after everything they've done for me.

So, deviating from my plan slightly, I find a blank slip of paper on Peepaw's desk and scribble out a quick note.

Thank you so much for everything.
I love you two very much,

*but I have some things back
home that I have to take care of.
I'm sorry to bail like this and
I hope someday I can come back.*

Love,
     Ell

    I leave sixty dollars on top as repayment for all the food I ate, and slipping the pen back in its place, I turn for the front door. Halfway across the living room, a weird sensation comes over me, my head swimming in circles. My stomach does a flip as I stumble forward, grabbing the back of the couch to steady myself. My vision narrows and I'm forced to the ground, my head slumping forward. It dawns on me that this isn't normal, but then voices fill my ears and my eyes roll back.

***

My head throbs as I open my eyes for the first time, and even though my vision still isn't right, it's immediately clear I'm not in Kansas anymore, or Meemaw and Peepaw's, *whatever*. I jerk my body forward, intending to stand up, but my hands are bound, and my ankles are as well. Panic sweeps over me as the fog in my head starts to dissipate. I twist my head, left to right as I take in my surroundings. The air is cool and smells like underground, and while I can barely see the wall behind me, it's obvious there are no windows. One door stands off to my right, big and metal and imposing, as if I'm trapped in here and the door is laughing at me. The only thing in the room with me is a bucket in the corner and a mattress that's seen better days lying next to it. If I was to guess, I'm in someone's basement, but why? Or, better yet, who's?

    I scream for help, but the only response is the *plop, plop, plop* from water leaking from the ceiling to the bucket. I yell so long my throat turns raw, my voice hoarse. I open my mouth to scream again, but I close it, feeling like a complete dumbass. Magic. Why didn't I think to use my magic? I swear, sometimes my stupidity amazes even me.

Reaching deep down for the magic I know is there, I wish these damn bindings off me. When a full minute passes and nothing happens, I shake my head and try again. Three more times and two other requests and still, nothing. My magic swirls inside me, but no matter how hard I try it just won't work. Of course, that doesn't stop me from trying for another hour in-between yelling for help. I'm so focused on making this work, I don't even hear the door creak open.

"It doesn't matter how hard you try, little Ell. Your magic is bound, and only I can undo it."

My head whips around, Jim's ugly Leprechaun face coming into view. I think somewhere in the back of my mind I knew he was responsible for my current predicament, but I just hadn't wanted to believe it. Well, there's no denying it now.

I grunt in his direction. "What the hell is going on? Why are you doing this?"

He chuckles at my demands, and with his hands clasped behind his back, he paces a line in front of me. "Well you see, I can't have another fairy in Electra. It would mess up all my plans, and we can't have that, now can we?"

"Listen, dude," I start, still wriggling my hands to try to break free. "I knew you were a Leprechaun and I didn't say shit. I'm not a threat to you." I pray that sounded convincing.

He shakes his head back and forth. "Tsk, tsk, tsk. I think we both know that isn't true."

"I swear," I try. "I left Fay for a reason. I just want to enjoy the life I've made here. I have no intention of messing with your best laid plans, or anyone else's, for that matter. Please, just let me go." Half of my plea was a lie, I'm just hoping he doesn't realize that.

"Oh, Ell," he says, stopping to face me. "Do you think I don't know exactly who you are?" He shakes his head as if I'm an utter disappointment. "I know you're the heir, sweet fairy. I know if my plan fails, your uncle will do anything to get you back. *You*, little one, are *my* backup plan."

He resumes his pacing, and I realize I am well and truly fucked. One-hundred percent, fucked. My only chance of surviving this little kidnapping was if he just thought I was any old fairy, but now that he knows I'm the heir, there is no way I live through this situation. Even if his plans fall through and he demands a ransom, I think I'll still die in the end.

"He won't pay the ransom. You know Seelie don't negotiate with terrorist-scum." I spit at his feet because, what does it matter? There's no reason to play nice now.

He looks at the wetness that hit the tassel of his loafer with disgust as he, "tsk's," me again. "Be very careful, *Princess*. I'll keep you alive as long as I think it's beneficial, but that doesn't mean that time won't be very, very painful for you. From this moment forward, your behavior will dictate mine." With a grunt, he storms from the room, slamming the door behind him, the wall shaking with the force.

Mother-flipping Leprechauns.

This is bad, really bad. Not only is there no way I live through this with my magic bound to that ass-hat, but my whole family might be wiped out. I know Jim wants Uncle Rowan dead, but why? What could he be plotting that he would need the King dead? I mean, short of a full takeover; I can't think of anything else. I guess a takeover isn't out of the question, but I have never in all my life heard of Jim, *or* seen him. Any fairies that are a threat to the Seelie are well known and well watched. Their faces have been burned into my mind since I was very young, so unless Jim is working for someone else, I doubt he's strong enough to kill the King and take over all of Fay. That's a lot of magic to wield. Not just anyone can handle it. I'm not even sure *I* can handle it, and I've been groomed for this.

The door lock clicks, starling me from my thoughts. When the door swings wide and a girl I don't recognize steps in, my immediate reaction is to beg for help. "Please, help me. My magic is bound, please."

For half-a-second a look of pity washes over her features, but as soon as it appears it's gone. She crosses the room without a word, deposits a tray in my lap and turns to leave. The door slams behind her, and I'm left alone again. Not only that, but what the hell was the point of giving me food if my hands are bound?

Assholes.

Minutes pass as I grow more frustrated because the food actually smells good. A half a dozen fresh strawberries, along with a big slice of meatloaf taunts me, as if that was Jim's reason for doing this all along. Make me suffer, knowing I can't eat it. Again I say, asshole.

A buzzing sensation starts near my lower back and I jerk, afraid of what's to come. But when the metal chain binding my hands loosens and falls to the floor, I jump to my feet, not caring that I just threw the food all over the floor. I rush to the door, trying the handle but it won't budge. Banging my fists against the hard metal, I pull back, hissing when I realize it's iron. My hands are on fire from the burn, so I resort to kicking the door instead with the toe of my boot.

"Let me the fuck out of here!" I scream until my voice cracks.

I rear back, kicking the door as hard as I can and I'm rewarded with a searing pain. The pain shoots up my shin and I wince. It only makes me hate Jim more, and I use it to fuel my fury. All of this is his fault, and I intend to make him pay.

"I swear to God, when I get out of here, I'm going to *fucking* kill you! Fucking piece of shit Leprechauns!"

I kick and scream until I can't anymore, my will to get out of here waning with my energy. Dragging my body to the dirty mattress, I slump in a heap, ripping a piece of my shirt before wrapping it around my singed hand. Fairies heal quickly compared to humans, so it won't hurt for long, but right now, it hurts like a son-of-a-bitch. Cradling it to my chest, I can't help but cry. I really hope Jim can't see me. I don't want to give him the satisfaction.

My whole body hurts now, and it's all Jim's fault. I meant what I said. If, no, *when* I get out of here, I don't care if he's the one to let me out, I'm still going to kill him. He's a dead-man-walking.

Tears track down my cheeks because I probably won't get that chance. My dad would say there's a lesson to learn here; that if I hadn't run away to Earth, none of this ever would've happened, and he'd be right. But if I hadn't, I never would have met Blake, and if this ends the way I think it will, I'll at least die happy knowing I made at least a few memories with him. And thank God I won't die a virgin. That's always been my worst fear.

I close my eyes, smiling as I think of last night. It was, hands down, the best night of my life and will hold the title for my favorite memory as long as I live. Yes, I realize that might not be long, but I'd like to think God will let me keep just one memory in the after-life. And if I get to choose, I have no doubt I'd choose last night.

I bet Blake is worried about me. I promised I would let him know before I left…

I gasp at that thought, remembering the note I left for Meemaw and Peepaw. No one will be worried about me. I left a fucking note. I was very clear that I was leaving and had things to take care of. So, while I'd like to think they're all sad that I'm gone, they most definitely won't come looking for me. Blake might stop by Meemaw and Peepaw's when he hasn't heard from me after a couple days. They'll show him the note and he'll have no reason to question it. He'll probably be pissed too. He'll be mad I didn't call, or at least text, and that will help him get over me.

I knew I was in a shit situation, but this clinches it. No one knows where I am, and since I can't help myself, there's now, officially, no way out of this.

SPIDEY SENSES

Blake

Last night was ridiculous. Honestly, I've had sex with my fair share of women, and none of those experiences even come close to last night. I'm sure some would say the difference is in sleeping with someone you love, and maybe that's true. I don't know, but what I do know is I can't live without that girl. Something told me that first night she walked in The Oasis that she would be mine, that she was meant to walk in to my life, and now that I've had her, I can't let her go. I know she has a past. I know she said I wouldn't feel the same about her if I knew, but I don't see how that could possibly be true. I also know she said she'd be leaving soon; that she didn't know if or when she'd be back. And while I should have told her this when I dropped her off at John and Midge's, I now know I can't let her leave. If she has to, then I guess I'll be going with her. Whatever she needs to handle back home, we'll handle it together.

  My resolve to convince her strengthens as I pull up the drive, John and Midge's little home coming into view. Bessie is in the driveway, so I know they're home, but that doesn't mean Ell is. I cut the engine and hop out, tossing the keys through the open window before straightening my spine and practically storming toward the front steps. Before I can reach the porch, John comes barreling out the front door, anger marring his features.

  "What did you do to her?" His question is a demand as he

bows up to me.

I tilt my head in confusion, not sure what he means. "John, I don't know what you mean. Where's Ell? What's wrong?"

His tone softens at hearing the fear in mine. "She...she's gone."

"What?" My voice raises a full octave as I strain to see past him into the house as if he's lying. "What do you mean she's gone? She promised to call me before she left."

The screen door creaks as Midge steps out, a slip of paper clutched tightly in her hand. "She left a note."

She thrusts the note toward me, and I don't hesitate snatching it from her grasp. I read it start to finish four times, not wanting to believe the words in front of me. This can't be real. She promised. I look up to John and then Midge, hoping they'll be able to elaborate, but seeing the look on each of their faces, I know this is all I'm going to get.

"She left," I whisper, the paper still clutched tight in my fist. I crumple it into a ball, and then straighten it out, knowing this might be all I have left of her. "Has she said anything to either of you, like where she's from or where she might be going? I know the note says she has things to handle at home, but has she said anything else?"

Midge moves forward gracefully, grasping my upper arm and tugging me forward. "Come inside, honey. Maybe we can think of something."

In a daze, I follow, praying she's right. Unfortunately, I have a horrible feeling in the pit of my stomach, and I can't seem to shake this thought that something is very, very wrong here.

***

Ell

I'm pretty sure I've been down here for a year. Yes, I know I'm being dramatic and it has only been a day, at best. Back off. I was kidnapped and I'm probably going to die down here, so cut me a little slack. This mattress smells like more than one person died on it, and the last food they brought me, I chunked on the floor. And fuck you if you think I'm eating off this floor. Meemaw's yes, this hell-hole, no.

No one has been in to see me in hours, not even the young girl that brought the tray of food. Through deductive reasoning, I've convinced myself that must have been around dinner time, which means they won't be back until breakfast. That is, assuming they plan to feed me three times a day. I know Jim wants me alive, but he could achieve that with feeding me very little, and it'll make it a lot harder for me to tell how long I've been down here. Not that it matters. I exhausted myself trying to break the binding on my magic. I should be stronger than him, so the fact that I can't undo the bind, says a lot about his abilities. Either that, or he's working with someone who's very, very strong. I've racked my brain at who it could be, but there's just no way to know.

Something tickles in the back of my mind and I scratch my head as if that will help. It feels like a fly or something buzzing around inside, and I can't imagine what would cause that. I guess that fuck-nugget could be screwing with me. If he thinks he can drive me insane, I've got news for him, too late buddy. I'm already bat-shit crazy.

I scream just for the hell of it. So what if I piss him off? I'm screwed anyway.

Sitting up, I pull at my ratty hair, and as it slips through my fingers, I notice my glamour is gone. I guess it makes sense. If my magic is bound, then I wouldn't be able to keep something like a glamour in place. Oh well, he knows who I am already anyway.

I let out a huff of annoyance at the itching sensation in my mind, and chunk the thin sheet across the room. I get up to pace, wracking my brain for some way out of this. I know there isn't one, but I need to pass the time. My boots hit the concrete floor over and over, the sound nearly driving me insane.

On the third lap around the room I freeze, the odd sensation in my mind turning to a whisper. It's definitely a whisper, but I can't make out the words or who it is. I don't know why, but something tells me whoever it is, they're worried. I'm just getting a vibe, don't ask me how. I've never experienced anything like this. Sure, there are fairies that can read minds or speak thoughts. It takes a special fairy to be able to do it though, and *I* am not the one.

The door swings open, startling me. I spin in a circle, mentally preparing myself for a fight. I let out a sigh of relief at seeing the young girl from yesterday, a tray in hand. When she sets it down just inside the door, never taking her eyes off me, I see the food she's brought suggests it's breakfast time. Good, at least now I know I can track the time.

"Please, just tell me how long I've been here." I don't move an inch, not wanting to scare her off. I place my hands out in front of me in a calming gesture, softening my features and praying she'll answer.

Pity shines in her eyes and I can see the minute she makes the decision. Leaning back, she glances down the hall both ways, and seeming satisfied we're alone, she turns back to face me. "You've been here since yesterday; late afternoon. I can't say anything else though. I'm sorry."

And with that, she shuts the door and I'm left staring at the iron monstrosity. I'm too hungry to wait too long, though, and once I'm certain the door won't open again, I rush to the tray, picking it up and scurrying back to my nasty mattress. Plopping down, I tuck my legs underneath my ass while popping a strawberry in my mouth. The juice flows down the back of my throat, soothing the raw walls and I moan. It feels *so* good. I finish off all but one strawberry, the one that looks the best, and move on to my scrambled eggs. Whoever prepared this meal took care with it. The eggs are still piping hot, and there's grated cheese mixed in along with grilled onions. I doubt Jim would do that. That means it's either the young girl, or someone else he's no doubt holding against their will. And to be clear, that girl is most definitely here against her will. I might not have been sure yesterday, but after seeing her fear as she decided if she should answer my simple question, there's no doubt in my mind now.

My mouth waters as I cram half a slice of buttered toast in my mouth, moaning again at how good it is. I wash it down with a swig of orange juice as I wonder where we could possibly be and how someone like Jim has slaves to do his bidding. Without my magic, I have no idea if that girl is a fairy. She could be an ordinary human for all I know. Although, that doesn't really make sense. Jim seems like the type to only keep people around who benefit him, and I can't imagine what he could gain from a human. Unless of course, it *is* about the cooking.

The only thing left on my tray is the best looking strawberry, and I stare at it longingly. I don't want to eat it. I mean, I do, but I also don't. I'm not starving or anything. It's just that eating helped take my mind off the slowly drifting minutes, and once that strawberry is gone, it'll be back to staring at the wall or pacing.

I pick up the plump, red fruit, gazing at the tiny black seeds. I saved this one specifically because it was the ripest and it looked extra juicy. Tell me you don't save one bite of the best tasting thing on your plate for the very end. If you say no, you're lying. I always save the best for last.

Did I mention, the oddest things flit through your mind when you're trapped in a basement with no end in sight?

With a shrug, I pop the fruit in my mouth, swishing it from one side to the other, trying to drag it out as long as possible. When it's mush in my mouth, I swallow, a tear slipping down my cheek. It isn't the fucking strawberry, although it might have been the best one I've ever had. It's my reality now. I wouldn't say I'm giving up, but I've always been a realist *and* a pessimist. A really bad combo, if you ask me.

I flop back, casting my arms out wide. I could really use some help from God right now. I mean, I know my ancestors were once angels, and God chose to leave them outside the pearly gates when he decided to close them, and while I don't know why, it couldn't have been good, but he must have some sort of good feelings toward us or he wouldn't gift us with the mark. I guess all that could be bullshit made up generation after generation. Hell, for all I know it could be magic an original fairy cast to ensure her line would remain in power and referred to them as the Seelie. Of course, that doesn't explain the mark of the Devil on the UnSeelie. Sure, it could all be part of the same magic or some long ago feud that no one remembers, but right now, I'd really like to think God favors me. I'd really like to think I'm important to him somehow, and that's why these stupid wings sit on my wrist.

A fat good they did me up to this point though.

That tickling sensation is back, pulling and pushing in the recesses of my brain. I try to latch on to it, but each time it's as if it slips through my fingers. I pray it really is something and not me going crazy, or worse, that I somehow managed to end up with a brain eating parasite. I watched a movie one time…

"Where are you, Ell?"

I know no one's in here, but I question the voice out loud anyway. "What the fuck? Who said that?"

The tickling in my brain stops, and wherever that voice came from, it's gone too. Now I'm left in an empty room with nothing but my thoughts, and *that* is a scary thing.

***

Blake

"I mean, she said she had to go home, so what makes you think something is wrong?" Liz questions me, clearly failing to feel as I do.

I throw my hands up in frustration as I pace the room for the hundredth time. "I don't know…okay? I don't know how to explain it, but I'm telling you something isn't right. She promised she'd call me before she left. And I'm sorry but there is no way she would up and leave John and Midge with nothing more than a one paragraph note."

"Okay, let's say that's true, then what could have happened to her that is so bad?"

I stop my pacing, sitting down hard in the arm chair in Liz's living room. Leaning forward, I drape my arms across my knees, clasping my hands tightly. "A couple days ago, Ell was at my house and Jim showed up looking for her."

"Is that the same day he up and closed the bar?"

"Yes," I confirm. "Which only makes the whole thing seem odder. When I showed up at work that afternoon, he sent me home, said he had stuff to take care of in Dallas. But then a few hours later he shows up at my house looking for Ell."

Liz bobs her head as if for the first time she might see what has me so concerned. "So not only was he not in Dallas, but he was looking for Ell, and at your place. Do you know if he went by John and Midge's looking for her, or did he automatically assume she was at your house? And if that's the case, how would he know to do that? It's not like everyone knows you two are a thing. In fact, I don't think anyone other than me, and I guess, John and Midge knows. Right?"

"Right. And no, I don't think he went out to their place. I don't know why, but I think he knew she was there, and that I was lying."

"Shit," she curses, rising from her seat before sitting back down again. "Let's assume that's true. What could Jim possibly have against Ell? I mean, they've only known each other since he showed up at the bar. Or am I missing something here?"

"I don't know. That's the part I can't work out. But whatever it is, I don't think it's just about Ell. I think Peg might be in danger too."

"Are your spidey senses tingling?" she jokes, but her face is serious.

"If that's what we're calling it."

She slaps a hand on each thigh before rising and leaving

the room without another word. Well, okay, I guess we're done talking. Getting up from my seat, I fish my keys from my front pocket and make my way to the door.

Opening the screen door, I get one foot outside when I hear Liz call from behind me. "Dude, don't leave me." She pushes past me, practically running to my truck. She jumps in the passenger side, slamming the door before calling for me to hurry. "Come on, Lassie. We haven't got all day. Our girl might be in trouble."

RANSOM VIDEO

Ell

A few hours of loneliness after breakfast, the same girl brought me lunch, and then a few hours after that she brought dinner. My internal clock says it's maybe been an hour since then, so I figure it's somewhere between 7:00 and 9:00 p.m. on day two. I haven't heard the voice again since breakfast, and trust me, I've tried to get it back. But no matter how hard I pull, it remains just out of reach. The itchy, tickling feeling is still there, although for some reason it feels further away.

The door swings open, slamming against the wall with a clang as I'm jerked from my thoughts. Jumping to my feet, I come face to face with two of the fairies I'd met that night in the bar, including the one that slapped my ass. God, I wish Blake was here right now, because without my magic, I don't stand a chance against these two. The tall and lanky one steps forward, a sneer on his face, and I take two steps back, nearly tumbling over the edge of the mattress. The other fairy remains near the door, while the tall one continues his advance.

"Aww, she's scared, Jas," he chuckles, and I'm pretty sure he's Melvin and the other one must be Jasper. That just leaves Borin unaccounted for. "Don't worry, pretty little fairy, we won't hurt you." And with a gleeful laugh, he adds, "Well, we won't *kill* you anyway. Not while the boss wants you alive."

"Stop playing with her," Jasper barks. "The boss wants

her upstairs, so let's go."

With a wiggle of his fingers, my head swims with magic and I fall. Pain streams through my body when I hit the ground hard. Melvin, the fuck-hole, didn't even bother to catch me. Chivalry is dead, y'all.

I'm conscious when he grabs me, a hand under each arm, and drags me unceremoniously out the door and down the hall. I try to take in my surroundings, but whatever Jasper did to me has left me with a splitting headache and tunnel vision. We turn a corner and I'm pretty sure we just passed the girl that brings me food, seated on a bed in a room that looks like mine, but I just can't be sure. When we take the next turn, I'm guided up a set of decrepit stairs, and at the top, Jasper quietly opens a closed metal door, Melvin and I following. Unless he's using some sort of magic, I'd say that door isn't iron, and I pray I can remember that later when this magic wears off. That information might just come in handy.

I'm dropped roughly on the carpeted floor, Melvin's boot connecting with my temple as he walks away. I feel the magic waning as I try to sit up, my limbs feeling like noodles. My head gradually clears, and I press my hand gently to the throb from Melvin's boot. I feel something wet, and pulling my hand away, I see blood. That son-of-a-bitch. I swear to God, if Melvin wasn't already on my list, he is now.

I growl, "You're black listed, *Melvin*."

I spot him on the other side of the room, his hands clasped in front of his stupid fucking crotch, and he cocks his head as if he doesn't understand what I mean. I shrug, flipping him off, and turn to survey the rest of the room. Holy shit, this is Peg's house. I'd recognize that ghastly floral chair anywhere. But why the hell does Peg have iron doors in her basement? I cringe, I may have seriously misjudged her.

A dark laugh assaults my ears and I turn. Jim sits casually on a couch against the far wall, his hands draped loosely between his open legs. He's wearing a yellowed dress shirt and chocolate brown slacks, looking like the Dwight of the group.

All he needs now is the glasses. Well, and I guess to lose the red hair. He leans back as he pulls his ankle up and sets it against his knee. He taps his thumb against his dirty, brown sock, and from the look of him, he's enjoying every minute of this.

"Ell, you are quite the spitfire, aren't you?" His tone is deep, and if I didn't know any better, I'd say he likes that I'm hard to deal with. Maybe it even turns him on, if the lust filled gleam in his eyes is any indication.

"Fuck you," I spit, finally able to stand. "Give me back my magic and fight me like a real fairy."

"Now, why would I do that?" he scoffs, slitting his eyes at me.

"You wouldn't," I growl, taking a step toward him causing Melvin and Jasper to move in my direction. "You wouldn't because you're a pussy."

I'm close enough that I see Jim's teeth clench, his jaw flexing at my name calling. I don't care though. I'd almost rather he kill me now. I don't think I can stay in that basement another minute.

Jim motions to Larry and Moe, and it has me wondering where Curly is. They flank me, with Melvin gripping my hair in his fist and Jasper securing my arms. I twist and turn, trying to pull away, but their grip only tightens and I'd bet my ass they're both having to use magic to keep me contained. I can almost feel it slithering over my skin. It makes me feel dirty.

My eyes cast toward the front door, the wooden rectangle no more than six feet away, and I just know if I could make it outside, I could get away. All I need to do is make it to the portal. The minute I step through I have no doubt the Seelie guard would be all over me like peanut butter on jelly. I'd be safe.

I try again to pull away, but Jim comes out of nowhere, backhanding me and sending my head careening backward. Immediately blood pours from my nose, and I mentally add another tick to his name. Keep rackin' 'em up, a-hole.

Jim grips my chin, pulling my head forward and I have

no choice but to look at him. "You're only making this harder on yourself, *fairy*. And don't even think about stepping foot out that door. I have barrier magic up anyway." His lids blink rapidly, and I'm pretty sure that's his tell. He's lying. He only wants me to think he has barrier magic in place.

"What do you want from me?" I growl through clenched teeth. "Why bring me up here?"

His grip loosens slightly as a sinister grin splits his face from ear to ear. "We're going to have some fun." He laughs, throwing his head back as if this is a game.

I wanna rip his stupid *con* face off. My teeth grind together, and I blow a breath out through my teeth.

"Put her on the couch, and shut her mouth until we're ready," Jim says, enraged.

Dick-less and Fuck-Nuts drag me to the couch, throwing me down and then I feel Jasper's magic slither over my skin again. It slides up my arms, leaving a sickly feeling in its wake. When it reaches my mouth, it turns wet, and with a gasp, my mouth is sealed shut. I rip and pull at the substance, trying in vain to free my lips. I cringe at the nasty feeling, but I know this shit won't come off until Jasper wills it so.

Giving up, I slump against the back of the couch, almost grateful to just be out of the basement. I watch as the three fairies move about the room, carrying various things here and there. When I see Jasper attach his phone to a tripod, I know immediately what's about to happen.

Monkey-fucker.

These fucks are about to make a ransom video, and I'm the star.

***

Blake

I fly down front avenue headed east, Liz in the passenger seat. We've already been to the bar, and finding it closed and the parking lot empty, we figured there was only one other place we could look; Peg's. I told Liz about mine and Ell's recon mission, and she'd seemed slightly impressed. I had, however, left out the part where I'd passed out due to a bee sting. I still find that a little odd. I mean sure, I've had an allergic reaction to a bee sting before, but I've never passed out. In fact, I can't remember ever passing out for any reason. But if I didn't pass out, then that means Ell lied, and I just can't bring myself to believe that. What purpose would it serve? It wouldn't. She had to be telling the truth. Hell, maybe it was one of those Africanized Bees.

I take a turn too sharp, my tires nearly leaving the pavement. Liz grabs the oh-shit-handle, a slew of curses leaving her lips. "Damn it, Blake. I sort of wanna live through the fucking day. *Fuck!*"

"Sorry," I mumble, tapping the brakes and bringing us back to a reasonable speed.

My hands clench the steering wheel, my knuckles turning white as I turn off the paved road and on to the first dirt road that will lead us to Peg's. The truck bumps along, and Liz finally lets go of the handle but grips her seatbelt tightly instead. The radio plays softly in the background, and I focus in on the words, trying to keep from flipping the fuck out. Yeah I know, it's a little late for that, but I need to keep it together until I confirm something bad has happened. But, mark my words, if I find out Jim had anything to do with Ell's disappearance, he's fucking dead. And while I have no evidence to prove his involvement, there's no doubt in my mind he is. He just better pray I find them before he touches one hair on her head, or I won't just kill him, I'll make him suffer.

***

Ell

A cell phone sits on a tripod facing me, while Melvin stands near the door to the basement and Jasper stands behind the phone. I assume he plans to operate the camera because Jim now sits way too close to me on the couch. His thigh brushes against mine, forcing a shiver of disgust to surge through my body. I nearly gag when his hand moves to rest on my knee, and I try to wiggle free but he won't let me.

"Now, Ell," he says, turning slightly in my direction. "We're going to make a video for your favorite uncle, and you're going to be a good fairy. If you aren't, we'll make the video anyway, and when we're done, I'll make you sorry you were ever born." With each word his hand on my knee squeezes tighter, and now I'm wincing at the pain. He lets go, giving me a pat before turning toward the phone setup and giving Jasper a thumbs-up.

Facing Jasper, I see him mouth, "Go," as he waves his hand for Jim to start.

Jim clears his throat, sitting up taller as he speaks. "King Rowan, you don't know me, but you will. I'm Jim Bicklaw...UnSeelie-marked by the Devil... a pure blood Leprechaun. As you can see, I've met your beloved niece. She and I have grown quite fond of one another." And turning to me, he adds, "Isn't that right, *dear*?"

I roll my eyes, trying to speak but only being able to growl my hatred. I wish he'd remove this stupid magic. I'd love to say a few things to the camera.

Jim turns away, facing forward, a grin of satisfaction perched on his lips. "Now, you must be wondering why I'm reaching out. See I had one plan, but now that Ell and I are so close, I have something else in mind. You have three days to kill yourself, King Rowan, but before you do, you'll issue a decree not only naming Ell as your successor, but you'll name me as her husband."

My eyes widen in shock, and I try with everything in me

to scream my denial. There is no way in the universe I'm marrying this piece of shit. Absolutely no way. I'll take a flying leap off the Empire State Building before I let that happen. There's no way Uncle Rowan would agree to this, right? Right. He would never. His utmost duty is to the people of Fay, even if he has to sacrifice his niece and heir to do it. If I die, he'll just have to rescind his retirement and wait on my little sister to come of age. He's retiring young by fairy standards anyway.

I jerk my head back and forth, hoping I'm conveying my disgust. Jim's hand grips the back of my neck tightly, causing a tremor of pain to shoot down my back, and I have no choice but to be still. My neck is stiff, eyes forward as I wait with bated breath to see what he'll say next.

"Three days, Rowan," Jim growls, disdain dripping from his lips as he fails to use my uncle's title. "Three days to do what I ask, and should you not..." His hand slides around my neck, running his grubby little paws through my hair. He produces a knife out of thin air, pressing it lightly to my throat, but the threat is evident. "Well, I think we both know what will happen if you deny me."

The video continues to roll as Jim leans in, sniffing me. That's right, the mother-fucker just sniffed me. So gross.

"Do you have anything you'd like to say, sweet fairy?"

What a dick move. He knows I can't talk. That... "Sorry, fucking piece of shit." Wait, was that out loud or did I just imagine it? My hand flies up, rubbing across my bottom lip and I find it clean, the sickly substance completely gone. When I open my mouth and whistle, a grin peeks through my lips. "Yes actually, I do have something to say." I smile sweetly at the camera before turning to Jim, keeping the smile plastered in place. "Fuck you!" I spit in his face, his only reaction a minor flinch.

He snaps his fingers and I know the video has ended. I also know I'm about to be in deep shit. He told me to behave, and I'm pretty sure spitting in his face doesn't count as good behavior. Oh well. I meant what I said, and honestly, it felt really good to watch my nasty spit splat on his ugly ass face.

Melvin and Jasper don't move from their positions, no doubt waiting to see what my punishment will be. Jim's hand moves and I barely manage to stop myself from flinching, but he doesn't reach for me. No, that sick fuck grabs his dick and repositions it. I don't know if it was me spitting in his face that turned him on or the promise of my punishment, but either way, it makes me sick to my stomach. The food I ate at dinner sours as he rubs his hand down his length twice, and I'm starting to regret my choices in life. I don't know how far he's willing to take this. I mean, a beating I can take, but what if he does more than that? I don't know if I could live through that.

He continues to stroke up and down his length as he turns to face me. "You should know, little fairy, that I'm double crossing one of my oldest friends by doing this. So if the King should deny me, I won't think twice about killing you to get back in with my friends in Fay, but just so you know, I'll make sure we all get to have a little fun with you before we send you to the afterlife."

I wish I could will him straight to hell as a moan gurgles up from the back of his throat and he snaps his fingers again. Melvin and Jasper move without question, snatching me up and moving back toward the basement door. I can't help but cast a quick glance over my shoulder, and seeing Jim still palming his dick, I shudder, causing Larry and Moe to let out an evil laugh. They drag me through the door and I trip going down. They let me fall, not even bothering to try to catch me. My head bounces on the concrete floor and I'm pretty sure I black out for a second.

The next thing I know, I'm lying on the floor of my room again, the door shut tight. I was really hoping I wouldn't end up back down here, but anything is better than being up there with Jim. I knew he was a bad guy, but I don't think I realized how bad until tonight. Although, I did get some valuable information out of the ransom video fiasco. What he said confirms what I've been thinking all along. Jim is, or I guess, was working with someone else. Probably someone who is much higher on the Un-

Seelie food chain. Whatever their master plan was, they needed to kill my uncle to accomplish it. And since Jim and his asshole friends are here in Electra, that means their end goal needed a lot of energy. I can't imagine what that goal is though, and who the guy at the top giving orders is. Could it be the UnSeelie King? He's really the only fairy that makes sense. But the problem with that theory; Jim doesn't strike me as the type to be friends with the UnSeelie King. Jim said he was double crossing one of his oldest friends, and there's no way you can make me believe Jim and King Tobin are besties. No way. But if not him, then who?

I guess it doesn't matter right now. He double crossed his so called, 'oldest friend' anyway. A double cross that leads me to the throne with Jim freaking Bicklaw at my side. Maybe it's best if I just die. If I don't, Fay will never be the same. The Seelie royal family has always protected all of Fay, despite the fact that there's a line drawn down the middle of the realm. The UnSeelie capital with their own royals, the Winter Court, and the Fall Court on one side, and the Seelie capital, along with the Summer and Spring Courts on the other. The UnSeelie, of course, don't recognize us as their monarch, but we believe we are tasked with protecting *all* fairies, regardless of their markings, or lack thereof. If an UnSeelie ends up crowned at my side, Fay might as well be called the Hell realm. They won't protect all fairies. They will only look out for their own, and all of Fay will descend into total chaos. Not to mention, they don't give a shit about the Earth realm, or the humans in it. Once they have control, they'll be free to come and go from Earth as they please, and with that much chaotic magic sweeping through Earth, there's no way it will stay intact. Earth realm will be destroyed if the UnSeelie rule Fay.

We can't let that happen. The problem is, I don't know how to stop it. I just hope my uncle is smart enough to know my life is not worth the destruction of Fay and Earth. Not to mention, the Heaven and Hell realms. They'll suffer too if my uncle doesn't stop this from happening.

This is so frustrating. I can't do anything to stop what I know is coming. I'm stuck down here in this stupid fucking basement with no end in sight. Without my magic, I'm only getting out of here if my dad somehow figures out where I am, and the chances of that happening are slim to none.

Being down here, trusting that other people like my uncle are making the right decisions, is one of the hardest things I've ever had to do. Weeks ago I didn't even want to ascend to the throne, but now, I wish I was already there so I could destroy Jim, his friends, and anyone else working with them. As it is, I have to put my faith in my family. My uncle is a smart fairy, and he's a good king. He *will* make the right decision. He has to.

THE SUCCUBUS OF THE FAIRY WORLD

Blake

I parked the truck about a mile out, and now Liz and I are traipsing through the same wooded area Ell and I did just days ago. The big hill comes into view, and as we climb, emotions war within me. On the one hand, I pray Ell's in this house because if she isn't, I don't know where else to look. On the other hand, if she is, I'm probably about to go to jail for murder. And while I'm okay with that if it means Ell is okay, I'm not really looking forward to maximum security with no conjugal visits.

I shake the thought away as we reach the top of the hill and, grabbing Liz, I pull her to the ground so we can get a look first. Our bodies press tight to a bed of grass, a bee buzzing dangerously close to me, and I hope we aren't about to have a repeat of the other day.

The sun is well past the horizon which doesn't leave us with a lot of light to see by, but I can just make out a light on in what I'm pretty sure is the living room. A car I don't recognize is parked in the driveway, right next to the old car I now know Jim drives. It's a piece of shit car, and since cars tell you a lot about a person, his choice doesn't surprise me.

I crawl another inch closer, thinking everything through. If Jim is telling the truth about being a friend of Peg's, and she did ask him to run the bar in her absence, then it makes sense she'd let him stay here while she was gone. The only problem with that is I've known Peg my whole life, and there is no way she wouldn't discuss something like that with her staff before she did it. Not that she would change her mind, just that she would have the decency to give us a heads up. Especially me, or at least that's what I think. I've worked in that bar in some capacity since I was sixteen. When Peg isn't there, I'm normally the one she leaves in charge. Why didn't she do that this time?

"Why is Jim even staying here?" Liz whispers, nearly scaring the shit out of me.

I nod. "Exactly.... come on, but stay low."

We crawl a few more feet before rising up to a squatting stance, staying low as we move closer to the back of the house. That weird feeling returns in the back of my mind, and I try to shake it away. It's been there for the last couple days, coming and going as it pleases, and I just can't figure out what it is. The weird part is, for some reason I associate it with Ell. I'm starting to think I might be losing it. In fact, a lot of weird shit has happened since I met her. Maybe it's just a coincidence, but I can't help but wonder.

When we reach the back of the house, we slide down the rough siding, our backs pressed tight against the wall just beneath the back window. If I remember correctly from the staff Christmas party last year, this window should give us a view of the eat-in-kitchen straight through to the living room.

Leaning in close to Liz, I press my lips close to her ear before whispering, "Just stay down, Liz. I'm gonna try to get a look."

Seeing her nod of confirmation, I swivel around, pulling my back from the wall and slowly rising to see over the windowsill. The curtains are pulled nearly closed, but whoever shut them left a tiny slit. I can just make out the couch, and squinting, I see one of Jim's cronies lounging on the center cushion.

I don't see Ell though. Part of me is relieved. The other part is livid because I realize I might never find her. I could be totally wrong about Jim. She really might have just gone home. And she really might never come back.

***

Ell

My head won't stop fucking ringing from the fall I took down the stairs. It left behind a knot the size of a baseball, and a wet patch I know is blood. I refuse to touch it though. That will only make the pain worse. I'm covered in scratches and bruises, and with each one I've made a mental mark next to the offender's name. I *will* get my vengeance. Mark my words.

I know it's getting late. I can feel it in my bones, and with each minute that passes, I am more certain Jim is about to come through that door. I don't know what he's waiting on, but I know before the night is through he's going to pay me a visit. And I guarantee I'm not going to like the way it goes. On top of that, that stupid itching is back, and now I know I'm going crazy. I have to be, because I'm pretty sure I just heard Blake talking to Liz. There's no way that's possible.

I hear a shuffle against the door and I move, rushing to the opposite side of the room. Here it comes. I don't know why I'm surprised. I totally called it. And when the door swings wide, revealing a smirking Jim, I'm pissed at myself for gasping. His grin only widens as he steps through the door, but I'm surprised when he doesn't shut it. I hope he doesn't think his stupid friends are going to watch. Absolutely not.

"You were a very, very bad fairy," he chastises me with a gleam in his eyes. A gleam that tells me he doesn't mind my bad behavior. In fact, I'm willing to bet he's grateful for it.

He takes two steps toward me and I feel the tendrils of his magic slip around my wrists, forcing me to stumble back. The magic tightens, seeping into my skin as I try to regain my footing. He lets out a cackle, and in one swift motion he's at my side, gripping my hair tightly. "Bad fairies have to be punished." His body presses against mine, and I try to pull away but it's no use.

Shit. Shit. Fuck. Fuck.

This is bad. This is really, really bad. He's not just going to beat the shit out of me, or punish me with magic, he's going to...

He drags me toward the door, the tips of my toes gliding against the concrete. He isn't even straining, so I have no doubt he's using magic. Leprechauns don't have much, but he clearly has enough to overpower me; at least with *my* magic suppressed. Still, since I know the magic he's using isn't the type of magic a Leprechaun would have naturally, I have to wonder who gave it to him. I'm guessing someone used their own magic to make his stronger.

I kick my legs back and forth, searching for purchase as he guides me up the stairs and down the hall. He lightly pushes Peg's bedroom door open, as if he doesn't have a care in the world, before depositing me on the floral patterned comforter. All I can think about is how fresh it smells, like a summer's rain.

I will the tears back as Jim shuts the bedroom door, and I realize there is no way out of this for me. I mean, I knew I was stuck in this situation short of a miracle but never, in all my skulking, did I imagine Jim doing something like this. If he doesn't physically kill me afterward, I have no doubt I'll be dead inside anyway. I know there are women who survive being raped and they come out stronger and better on the other side, but I'm not the one. I won't survive this.

Jim stands at the door, his demeanor relaxed as he stares at me lying prone on the bed. "You will make a fine wife, little fairy." He begins unbuttoning his shirt, one torturous button at a time. "Tell me, even with your magic suppressed I can't tell, what type are you?"

I don't want to tell him; it'll only turn him on more. Nymphs are practically the succubus of the fairy world. As far as someone like him is concerned, he just hit the fairy jackpot.

Seven. Seven. Seven.

When I don't answer right away he makes a "tsk'ing" noise

in the back of his throat. "Tell me, and I promise to make sure you enjoy this."

"There's zero chance of that happening, asshole. But if you must fucking know, I'm a Nymph."

The shiver that racks his body is visible even from here, and it causes a different sort of shiver to run through mine. His shirt falls to the floor, but he doesn't remove his pants as he takes a few languid, almost drunk steps toward me. I can practically see the triple-sevens in his eyes.

"Hmm," he hums. "This couldn't have turned out better for me. I always knew the Devil favored me." His eyes cast up and down my body, spending more time on my chest than anything.

I shake my head, crawling back on the bed and wedging myself against the window frame. "Are you stupid? There is no way my uncle is going to meet your demands. But he will hunt you down like a dog and torture you for the rest of your miserable fucking life. And surely you know that if you go through with what you're about to do, he won't just kill you when he finds you. He's going to make you suffer. He could make you suffer for an eternity, ya know."

"We'll see about that." He sounds totally sure of himself as he continues to peruse my body.

His knees hit the bed frame, his hand undoing his belt and I look to the window, wondering if I can make it out before he gets to me. There's less than three feet between us, so it's unlikely, but I have to try something. Maybe I should play along, let him think I'm into it and then strike. Yeah, that's probably a smart move. I know I said I wanted to make him suffer, and I do, but first I need to get out of this situation. I need to make him suffer on *my* terms, not on his.

My brain itches as I press myself harder against the window frame. *"Stay here, Liz. I'm gonna check out the other side of the house."*

What the hell?

I scratch the back of my head, trying to get rid of the incessant itching and Blake's voice in my mind. I'm not sure why or how, but I'm definitely hallucinating. I must have hit my head one too many times in the last few days. Or maybe this is my mind's way of escaping reality.

The buckle of Jim's belt clangs against the metal bed frame, pulling me back to the present. When his pants drop to his ankles, revealing a pair of dirty tighty-whities, I make the decision. I'm going to play along until the time is right, and then I'm going to kill this shit-stain, and if I can't kill him, I'm going to get the fuck out of here.

Taking a deep breath and willing my fear away, I relax, forcing what I hope is a sexy smile on my face. "Promise it'll be good for both of us?"

"Oh yes, little fairy. You have my word."

He places one knee on the bed, the mattress sinking with his weight. He moves to climb on fully, but before he can, the window above my head shatters, glass cascading down as I duck.

***

Blake

I'd watched as Jim's crony rose from the couch before disappearing out of sight. I crawled over to the kitchen window, but my view had been blocked fully by the curtains. Returning to Liz, I'd warned her to stay put, and then I crab-walked slowly around the house, looking for another viewpoint. I knew Peg's bedroom was toward the front of the house, in the far corner, so I'd worked my way in that direction assuming based on the time, anyone inside was most likely in bed.

When I'd rounded the corner, that nagging sensation was back and I don't know what it was, but something told me Ell was close. I could almost feel her energy inside me being drawn to her, as if we are somehow linked. Just one more thing to add to the list of weird shit going on lately.

When I'd reached the window I was pretty sure would

give me a view of Peg's bedroom, I heard a low murmur. I strained to hear and could just make out Jim talking to someone, but to who, I wasn't sure. That is, until I peeked over the windowsill. Nothing could have prepared me for seeing Jim stripping, or seeing the back of Ell's head pressed tight to the window frame. Her hair was purple though, which was odd, but there was no doubt in my mind it was her. I'd recognize her anywhere, even just the back of her head.

Even now, as I slump against the siding, my breathing erratic, I'm not sure what I just witnessed. Is Ell fucking Jim? How could she? I mean, I guess we've only known each other for a short time, but I don't think I imagined her feelings for me. Not to mention, she hates Jim. There is no way she's been sleeping with him the whole time. Right?

I let out a quiet sigh because, honestly, I don't know that for sure. That *would* explain why he showed up at my house looking for her, and why she acted so weird the last few days. Maybe she was already sleeping with him before me, and she didn't know how to tell me.

Does she love him? I can't imagine him being her type. He's old compared to her. Plus, Ell is legitimately the hottest girl I've ever seen in my life and Jim, well let's just say I figure Jim got hit with the ugly stick a few too many times at birth. On top of that, Ell told me she loved me. Either she lied, or I've got this whole situation wrong. But I just don't think that's the case. She looked straight at me when she confessed her feelings, and there was nothing in her eyes that suggested she wasn't telling the truth. I felt it in her words, and in everything that happened after.

I scrub my hand down my face as I hear Ell speak, "Promise it'll be good for both of us?"

Fuck.

I hear a twinge in her voice, something like hesitation and worry, and I'm certain this is against her will. I search my surroundings for something to break the glass, and coming up empty, I use the next best thing. My fist.

***

Ell

I'm curled into a ball, glass raining down on me still as I cover my head with my hands. I hear someone yell, but I'm not sure who and everything seems far away, as if it's in slow motion. Then without warning, everything comes rushing back. And I do mean everything. It's like I've been stuck in a vortex for the last two days, and I'm just now finding my way out. My magic isn't back fully, but I can feel it stirring around as a body goes flying over me. I jerk my head up, and seeing Blake on top of Jim, raining punches left and right, I nearly pee myself in excitement. God, I hope this isn't a hallucination. That would really suck.

Energy pours into me, pushing me back. I fly off the side of the bed with the force and it takes me a second to get my bearings. I can almost *see* magic or energy, I'm not sure which, leaving Blake and racing toward me. I feel full and strong as I stand over the two as they fight.

After what just happened, you wouldn't think I'd be thinking about sex right now, but apparently there's something wrong with me. I feel that tell-tale ache watching Blake's bicep flex as he clenches his fist and rears back for another punch.

Shaking thoughts of sexy-time away, I pull what magic I can find together and prepare to use it. I don't want to hit Blake, but I also need this to be over. We can't take any chances on Jim getting the upper hand. If he does, not only will he have me, but he'll have Blake too. And, I'm pretty sure Liz, since it seems I wasn't hallucinating earlier.

I don't have enough magic yet for a binding, but I do have enough to knock him out, I think. But before I can send the magic Jim's way the door bursts open. Well, there's Curley. I've been wondering when he was going to show up.

Disappointed I don't get to knock Jim out just yet, I

change my trajectory, aiming everything I've got at the three stooges standing in the doorway, looks of shock sweeping over their faces. My magic lets loose, soaring across the room and knocking two out of the three into the hall. I don't know if they're down for the count, but I'm really hoping they are. I just gave them nearly everything I had. I don't know how much more I can do. I can already feel my magic slipping away again as I stumble to the side. A thud draws my eyes back to Blake, and I'm shocked to see Jim is now on top of him. That could only mean Jim used magic on him because, in a fist fight, Blake wins every single time.

I race the few steps to their side, narrowly missing a whizzing ball of magic Melvin just threw my way. I take what I have left, and turn the magic back, his hair singing on contact. He lets out a yelp, stumbling backward, his head hitting the doorframe. Hopefully that nasty head wound will keep him occupied for a few because, from the looks of it, Blake is losing badly. I watch as Jim adds magic to his punches, his fist surrounded in an aura of red. I doubt Blake could see it even if he wasn't starting to lose consciousness, but I damn sure can. Cheater.

Blood pours from Blake's nose, and his bottom lip is split clean open. There's a cut above his right brow, and his hair is matted with blood, which means there's a wound in his hairline that I can't see. I add a bunch of ticks next to Jim's name, burning Blake's injuries to memory as I move as close as I can.

Whatever binding magic they put on me must have been strong, because my magic has never really needed time to charge before, but here we are, so I need to figure out a way to buy some time. I search the room, coming up empty, but then my eyes land on a canary-yellow lamp. I race for it, ripping the cord from the wall and turning back to Jim. I hear an ear-splitting screech from down the hall, but I don't slow, smashing the porcelain over Jim's head and watching him tilt sideways.

Well, that maybe bought me a minute.

EX-NAY ON THE MAGI-CAY

Ell

I was right. That damn lamp bought me exactly sixty seconds, but what bought me even more was Liz's crazy ass. I swear she has Banshee somewhere in her line. That girl came screaming down the hall, and I'm pretty sure busted everyone's ear drums, including my own.

Unlike me, she'd brought a real weapon to the fight, a butcher knife in her hand as she careened through the door, slashing left and right. She'd gotten Melvin a few times, and on the last, he'd scrambled down the hall, hurrying to get away from the psycho with a knife.

She'd yelled after him, *"That's right. Run like a little bitch,"* and I'd never been so damn proud in my whole life. I knew I liked that girl. I'm definitely going to keep her.

Right smack dab in the middle of a life threatening moment, I'd taken the time to pull her in for a hug. Apparently, Blake had not been amused, chastising us both. But I think it had all been for show because he stumbled toward us before pulling both of us in close.

Unfortunately, the fight wasn't over. While Melvin had run for the hills, Jim and Jasper had both come to. They clearly thought they were going to win this fight, because they didn't think twice about using magic in front of two humans. I'd barely been able to stop it with a discreet flip of my wrist. What? I'm not ready for Blake to know yet, okay? Geez.

Now though, I don't think that's an option because as Blake stands in front of Liz and I as if he's the only one who can protect us, Jim and Jasper stand side-by-side on the opposite side of the room. There's no way they aren't planning on using magic to win this, and if I don't use mine, then they've got this in the bag. You can't bring fists to a magic fight. Although, Blake did a damn good job of holding his own thus far. Also he's hot, so he can do no wrong in my eyes.

Jim cracks his neck left and then right as Jasper grinds his fist against his other hand. So cliché. I'm *so* rolling my eyes right now. It's like if you wrote a book about all the things men do to look intimidating when they really aren't, these two fuck-wads would be on the cover.

The air around me changes, and I know this fight is about to resume. I was really enjoying the respite. It's Jim who makes the first move, but I see it coming as he favors his left side. From behind Blake, and with Liz on my right, I'm able to stop whatever he threw Blake's way. I'm not sure what he planned to happen, but it's dead in the water halfway across the room. His second attempt, however, isn't aimed at Blake, and while I manage to weaken it, I'm not able to stop it completely. It hits Liz in the chest, her legs flying over her head as she careens across the room. She lands with a sickening thud against the wall, and I pray that doesn't leave any permanent damage. I hear her moan and sigh in relief as I come to a decision. I'm playing defense right now in an attempt to avoid being found out, but if I keep that up, we *will* lose. I need to be on the offense, not the other way around.

When Blake growls and charges forward, I recognize this as my chance. He has his back to me and I'm pretty sure Liz is still mostly unconscious. Tugging on the energy link between my chest and Blake's, I roll it all up into a tiny little ball, and pray a little vision magic works. It doesn't always, and sometimes it backfires. We really can't afford for that to happen, so I mentally cross my fingers and toes.

With a glance toward the hall, I see Borin is completely out, so while Jim and Jasper are preoccupied with the bull charging their way in the form of my hot boyfriend, I take my chance, throwing my magic with a thought and hoping it sticks. I barely have time to develop the vision before I release, and when it hits Jim square in the chest, I don't think it worked at first. Blake smashes into him and the two go flying out the doorway and into the hall, while Jasper looks almost surprised. Knowing I missed him with my magic all together, I scramble for just a little more. This house is jacking with my mojo. If I had all my magic, this would've been over ten minutes ago.

Preparing to throw a little sleep magic his way, I freeze when I hear Jim singing. It's barely audible over the sound of Blake's fists connecting with flesh, but I can just make it out.

"*Hallelujah...Hallelujah...Hallelujah, Hallelujah, Hallelujah.*"

O. M. G. This is too funny. This Devil-marked clown is singing a Christian hymn. This might be the new best moment of my life. I sure wish I knew where my phone was. This would get a million views easy. I bet God is really enjoying this.

My eyes cast toward the ceiling and I say out loud, "You're welcome," before turning back to where Blake still sits on Jim's chest.

Blake's fist freezes mid-air as Jasper looks on in confusion. I almost forgot about the sleepy-time magic I had ready, so while Jasper is preoccupied, I discreetly let it fly. He turns his head at the last second but it's too late. My magic taps him on the nose before sinking under his skin and settling. The energy around him turns a pale shade of blue as his eyes become droopy. I didn't have a lot left in me, so I doubt it knocks him out fully, but hopefully it's enough to buy us some time. He weaves left and then right, as he bumps into the wall softly.

Turning back to Blake who now sits straddling Jim, his fist still raised in the air, I wonder what he thinks about all this. I doubt his first thought is someone is using magic, but how else do you explain all the bat-shit crazy that just went down? Hell, that's *still* going down.

Blake's arm drops to his side as he leans back on his haunches. Jim is still singing, but now he's switched to an old Elvis Presley song. I could actually get into it if the fairy could even remotely carry a tune. As it is, his voice cracks with every high note he tries to hit as he sways his head to the beat and snaps his fingers.

Blake stands, looking between Jim and Jasper, two looney-tunes in a pod, and I make my way over, what little magic I have left at the ready. Passing Blake, he opens his mouth to speak, but I give him my index finger and don't look back. I hope I didn't hurt his feelings, but this shit isn't over. He may not realize that, but I do.

Stepping past Jasper and over Jim, I make my way to the basement door before stomping down the stairs. What we need is some iron bindings or anything that I can turn into a binding with a little magic. And the only person who might actually be able to help us is somewhere down this dark and dank hallway.

My hand runs along the wall, searching for a light switch but I come up empty. There's a light at the end of the hall, but it's not doing much to light my way. I hate to admit how scared I am right now, and it's a good thing Tab isn't here, she'd never let me live it down.

Too scared to go any further, I holler, "Hello?"

Only silence answers my greeting, and I wonder if the girl managed to get away during all the fighting. I certainly wouldn't blame her if she did. I'm not even sure how she ended up here in the first place.

The hall is lined with doors, three on the left and four on the right, so it's possible she and I weren't the only ones being held captive. Once again, I'm reminded that this is Peg's home not Jim's. Is it totally weird to have seven rooms in your basement? Maybe not. But it is weird to have seven rooms closed off with massive iron doors. Even if the iron has nothing to do with fairies, why does she need to secure these rooms? I know Blake and Liz grew up around Peg, but it's becoming more and more obvious that as far as Peg is concerned, there's a lot we don't know. Once we make sure she is, in fact, okay, she has a lot of explaining to do.

A squeak toward the end of the hall has me jerking back, nearly stumbling over something in the floor. I steady myself, and when I don't hear it again, I call, "Hey, I'm not gonna hurt you. I just need your help. The three blow-hards are down for the count. You don't have to worry about them."

A head peeks out from a doorway halfway down the hall, and I nearly shit myself. Seriously, I've been holding it for two days, refusing to go in a damn bucket. Oh, like you would. Pa-lease.

The girl's hair hangs down across her face as her eyes scan the area for any threats. She looks ragged and terrified, and I instantly feel sorry for her.

"Seriously, they aren't down here. One ran off, one is unconscious, one is suffering from a little case of the sleepys, and the other, well, the other you'll just have to see for yourself."

The girl takes a step into the hall, and I realize she might be younger than I thought. Originally, I had placed her at around sixteen or seventeen, but now, now I'm thinking she may barely even be in her teens.

"How did you do it?" she asks, and I'm not sure what she means. "How did you get your magic back?"

I sigh, pursing my lips. "Honestly? I'm awesome." She tilts her head to the side as if she thinks that's a legitimate answer. Clearly she doesn't get sarcasm. "I had a little help from some friends. It's safe though. I swear. But we need some bindings to make sure it stays that way. Know where any are?"

She nods her head, turning and walking to the far end of the hall. She opens a small door on the right, and squatting down, she digs around inside. She seems to find what she's looking for, and standing up, she kicks the small door shut with her toe before making her way to me, three sets of iron cuffs in hand.

She hands them to me and I nod. "That'll do, pig."

Her eyes grow wide, and she seems hurt. Again, I'm going to have to be real when I talk to her. "Oh my God. It's from a book. I wasn't calling you a pig or anything. Well, actually I did, but that's not what I meant. You know what? Forget it. Let's go."

I turn, not waiting to see if she'll follow, making my way upstairs. When I get to the top, I hear her soft footsteps behind me, and leaving the door open for her, I head down the hall to where I hope things are still in control.

***

Ell

Nearly to the end of the hall, I panic when I don't see at least half of Jim's body in the hallway. Picking up the pace, I sprint through the door and am relieved to find Jim and Jasper curled up in a ball together on the bed. Jim has his arms wrapped around Jasper, singing him a lullaby, and Jasper can barely keep his eyes open. Blake kneels down near Liz who's just starting to come to, and both of them look at me when I step in the room.

"Where did you go?" As soon as the question leaves Blake's mouth, his eyes widen and turning, I see the girl has followed me in.

I really should ask her name. It feels kind of weird at this point to just keep calling her "the girl". I mentally shrug, because there'll be time for that later, and turn back to Blake to answer. Holding the cuffs in the air, I explain, "Found these. Figured they might come in handy."

Not waiting for him to respond, I cross to the bed, being sure to position my body just right so Blake won't be able to see what I'm doing. My magic is doing much better now that I've had a little break, and I'm going to need it. I could just put the iron cuffs on both of them, sans magic, but that would put on a show that I'm not sure I could explain. The iron will burn their skin so violently that it won't matter that Blake and Liz aren't fairies. I need to avoid that, so I'll have to place a small amount of magic between the iron and their skin. Then I'll bind the cuffs to my own magic, that way no one will be able to take them off but me. Well, unless they have a fairy friend that's stronger than me, but let's not worry about that right now.

I place the cuffs on Jim first since he's the most awake right now. I click one cuff and then the other in place as I feel the girl brush against my side.

When she speaks, I startle. "Wow, how much magi…"

I elbow her in the side, turning my head just slightly to try to get her attention before whispering, "Ex-nay on the magi-cay. *Damn.*"

Her hand flies up, covering her mouth as she realizes her mistake. I mean, she couldn't have known but damn it. I'm in the homestretch right now, and I'm not opposed to slapping a bitch if she fucks this up for me. You know what, I really shouldn't call her a bitch. I'm pretty sure she's basically a child.

I sigh as I slip the second set of cuffs on Jasper. "What's your name?"

I don't think she realizes I'm talking to her, but when I give her a look, her mouth opens in an O. Finally, she says, "My name is Sasha."

"Okay Sasha, leaving out certain details, how did you end up with these three clowns?"

As she talks, I rush into the hall, placing the third set of cuffs on a still unconscious Curly, a.k.a. Borin. "Aife took me from my parents when I was ten as payment for taxes in the Winter Court." She fidgets with the hem of her worn blouse, and I instantly feel protective of her.

Leaning over Borin's prone body, and with a quick glance to make sure no one is watching, I bind the cuffs on his wrists to my magic. He doesn't budge, and wiping my hands off on my thighs, I quickly move back to the bed.

Back in the room, I swirl my magic around and around Jim and Jasper's cuffs, topping it off with a little connection magic. "Who's Aife?"

"They call him the taxer," she explains, quietly. "He's the one who collects the taxes in the Winter Court."

"What's the Winter court?" Blake's voice shocks me, not realizing he'd moved closer. "And what the hell happened to your hair?"

Well, double fuck me. How the hell do I explain this? I shoot my head at Sasha, even though this isn't her fault, and the guilt that sweeps across her face makes me feel bad. I need to remember this girl has been through hell and back, instead of being a bitch to her. None of this is her fault. If I had been up front with Blake in the first place, it wouldn't matter what Sasha said, or that my hair is somehow miraculously lavender. This is what I get for lying, but it's not like I had a choice, and even still, I can't bring myself to tell him. I'm just too exhausted. Yeah, that's the reason. *Whatever*, Ell.

My thoughts flit back and forth as I try to come up with a halfway believable answer to Blake's questions. "The Winter Court is a British thing." I hold my breath, waiting to see if he'll argue, but all he does is give me a, "*huff*."

"And the hair?" he questions again, eyeing me suspiciously.

"Yeah, that would be his fault," I blame, pointing at Jim.

Blake leans in, brushing his lips against my ear. "I like it."

A warm, fuzzy feeling rolls through my body as he steps back, and I blush as Sasha watches the exchange. She is way too young for the things I'm imagining doing to Blake. This whole situation has been very stressful, and I hear orgasms are excellent stress relievers. I'm going to need eighty-seven of them, at least.

Liz appears near Sasha, putting her arm around the skittish girl. "So he kidnapped you and kept you all this time?" And seeing Sasha's nod of confirmation, she adds, "How old are you, sweetie?"

"Fifteen."

Liz croons, "Oh honey, come on. Let's get you out of here."

Liz guides her from the room, leaving me with the bumbling idiots and a very suspicious Blake.

***

Blake

Ell stands with her back to me, looking more than a little worse for wear as Liz exits the room, Sasha clutched tight to her side. Jim, and whoever the other guy is, lay in a heap on the bed, Jim singing a show tune, while the third guy lies in a ball just outside the bedroom.

I'm not really sure what just happened here. More than a few things happened in the last twenty minutes that have me scratching my head. How did Liz get chunked across the room when no one was anywhere near her, and why in the hell did Jim start arbitrarily singing while I was in the middle of beating the shit out of him? Did I break him? And then there was the comment that Sasha made about some Winter Court. It wasn't so much what she said, as it was how Ell reacted to it. I don't know a lot about Great Britain, but I do know the Winter Court isn't British. It kind of makes me wonder if this has something to do with Ell's past, her home. I don't know. It's all just weird. And what's even weirder, is how she hasn't moved from her spot, hovering over the two men in the bed, refusing to even look at me. Is she mad at me? And if so, why? And don't even get me started on her hair. So Jim is a kidnapping rapist and he what, dyes his victim's hair? I don't buy it.

I retrieve the memory from shortly before I busted the window out, Ell's words causing the need to force down a growl. She made him promise it would be good for both of them, so does that mean she wanted this, or I guess, *him*? I can't even imagine a world where that's possible. I mean, Ell is, well, *Ell*. And Jim is a disgusting pile of dog shit. The two do not go together. I guess there's only one way to find out what the fuck just happened here, but I'm really dreading the answers. What's worse; the realization that Ell may have been lying to me this whole time, and when I ask her to explain everything that just went down, there's a real chance it'll be more lies. I don't want to believe that, but how else do you explain her behavior?

My hand brushes down Ell's back, and she flinches, making my stomach turn sour. "Ell, look at me, please." When she doesn't turn right away, my chest constricts, the air refusing to flow as it should. "Ell, please."

I barely get my plea out when she turns, worry in her eyes. "Blake, it's not what you think."

"What do you think I think?" I ask with a chuckle, trying to ease the tension in the room.

"What *do* you think?" Her head cocks to the side as she turns to face me more fully.

"I don't know what I think. But...I'm wondering if you're fucking the new boss."

She gasps, her hand flying toward me before forming a fist and punching me square in the chest. "*Ew*, how dare you! I would never. I can't even look at you right now." She spins, but I stop her.

I can't describe how big the sigh is that I let out at her words. "Thank God. I really was worried that you were..." I can't even finish that statement.

Her expression softens as she takes a step toward me, her hand rubbing the spot she just hit. I slip my hand around hers, pulling it to my mouth and placing a soft kiss on her palm before dropping it back to its original spot.

"Tell me what happened," I beg, hating how desperate I sound.

Her head falls forward, her forehead resting on my chest, and I grasp the back of her head, holding her tight. When I feel a sob rack her body, I lose it, picking her up bridal style and carrying her from the room.

Explanations can wait.

NO CHOICE

Ell

My sobs had not been a ploy to misdirect Blake's attention. I didn't do it to keep from having to explain everything to him. I swear. Although, it was an added bonus. No, those tears had been very, very real. The last two days have been a living nightmare, and when he asked me to explain, the first thing that popped in my brain was that I had come this close to being raped. Even now, as Blake lies next to me in my bed at Meemaw and Peepaw's, I can't stop the shiver of disgust that passes from my head to my toes.

Blake snores lightly next to me, his arms encasing my sore and tired body. Everything aches. Every single inch. But on the plus side, my magic is back in full force. In fact, it was back as soon as we had gotten ten feet away from Peg's house. Whatever magic Jim had used to suppress it, only applied inside a small bubble that surrounded the house where he'd kept me. Thank God. I was really starting to worry I might never be the same. Luckily, that isn't the case, and actually, I think my magic might be stronger. Don't ask me how, but I know without a doubt it has to do with Blake. Even now, I can feel the energy streaming from him to me. It's like the minute we slept together, I got an upgrade. Hey, I'll take it. I think it's going to come in handy, because whatever just went down with Jim, isn't the end. Sasha even mentioned some fairy named Aife, and if he's associated with Jim, then he's probably in on Jim's plan to kill my uncle. Granted, Jim said he had a new plan, but whoever he was working with doesn't know that yet. Maybe I was wrong about him working with King Tobin, maybe it's this Aife character. Maybe Aife is the fairy pulling the strings. Regardless, I need to get home and warn my uncle. But first, I need to figure out what to do about Jim, Jasper and Borin, not to mention find Melvin. I'm pretty sure those cuffs and the connection magic I used will hold. Plus, as we were leaving, I placed a barrier on the house, but Melvin is still unaccounted for which makes my skin crawl. On top of all that, I need to help Sasha get home to her family. She hasn't seen them since she was ten. I can't imagine what that's like. She's at Liz's for now, but when I leave to head back to Fay, I'm taking her with me.

Blake stretches, startling me as he lets out a yawn. "Why didn't you wake me?" He tugs me to him, forcing my head against his chest.

"You were really sawing logs," I giggle. "I figured you could use the sleep." And also, I'm putting off having to explain the last two days, but I don't tell him that.

"If you're awake, I'm awake," he says, bopping me on the nose playfully. Yawning again, he pushes me to the side before crawling off the bed, leaving me immediately cold. "I'm gonna grab some tea. Want some?"

I nod my head in the affirmative, and enjoy myself as I watch his fine ass strut out of the room. He wasn't even trying. But damn, he looks good. If there's an award for finest ass, he should win it every single year.

Seconds later he returns, two glasses of ice-cold sweet tea in hand. Sitting up, I pull my knees to my chest, thrusting my hands out in a give-it motion. "Gimme. Gimme."

A chuckle leaves his sexy, plump lips as he hands me the glass before claiming a seat on the edge of the bed. "John and Midge left a note. Said Midge had a doctor's appointment and they wouldn't be back until late this afternoon."

"Okay." I take a big swig of the diabetes in a glass, savoring the cool liquid as it slides down my parched throat. "I smell."

He chuckles again, but then his features change. "Should we shower?"

I use my best southern accent as I bat my lashes. "Why, Blake Black, what kinda girl do you take me for?"

He raises one brow, reaching for my tea and snatching it out of my vice-like grip.

"O.M.G. What kind of person steals a girl's sweet tea?"

"Hush," he orders, soft and yet somehow firm as he sets his glass and mine on the bedside table.

Leaning over, he hoists me on his shoulder and hurries toward the bathroom. I squeal as he kicks the door open before giving my ass a firm smack. The noise echoes through the small space, and my anticipation builds. Heat forms in my fairy-bits, and I pray this leads where I think it is. Setting me down on the counter next to the sink, he whips his shirt off, chunks it at my face, and hurries to the shower before turning it on. Testing the temperature and seeming satisfied, he flicks a few drops of water in my direction before stripping the rest of his clothes off. Once they're in a pile on the floor, his haste ceases, his sauntering ways returning. I give him my best come hither look, and I know my eyes are teaming with lust. Blake places a hand on each of my knees before spreading my legs apart enough to allow him access. Slipping in-between, he moves one hand around to my lower back, pressing me flush against him before removing my shirt and bra in a flash. Seriously, how does he do that?

"I was so worried about you," he says, his tone laced with concern.

"Blake, you're ruining the moment," I joke. But seriously, he is. Let's focus.

He nods. "You're right. That can wait. But, I don't think we're quite dirty enough for a shower."

"Oh really?" I toy with the button of his jeans, his abs looking very lickable.

"Really."

His hands rest on either side of me, boxing me in as he lowers his head to my breast. His tongue flashes out like a bolt of lightning, lapping at my perky nipple. My hands grip the back of his head as he moves to give my other breast a little attention. The rough surface of his tongue feels amazing and I throw my head back, my clit aching for a little attention too. His mouth leaves my nipple, the wetness left behind turning cold with his absence. He peppers kisses down my stomach, stopping just above my waistband as his fingers begin to undo the button. The button releases with an audible pop as he stands, wrapping his arm around my middle and lifting me. He shimmies my jeans down, but leaves my panties and I have to repress the whine that threatens to tumble out. My ass hits the cold counter, a shiver jolting through me as he lets me go to remove my jeans now trapped around my ankles. I expect him to get back up, but instead he kneels before me, a wisp of beautiful brown hair slipping across one eye. He sweeps it back in place as he leans forward, his tongue jutting out and making a long lick down my panties.

I shudder, "Oh, God."

My heart is pounding when his hand runs along the inside of my thigh before pulling my panties to the side. I've never done this before, so I find my nerves ratcheting up a notch, but I'm mostly ecstatic. I don't know if he's about to use fingers or tongue here, but I am *so* for it.

Oh God, he's using both.

His index finger penetrates *my girl* as he makes one long sweep from bottom to top with his tongue. At the top, he finds my clit, swishing the tip of his tongue from left to right. Over and over and over and oh my God. I can't help the scream that forces through my lips when he pumps his finger in and out, and I know I'm about to come. When he adds a second finger, making me feel even more full, an embarrassing noise trickles out of my mouth, my eyes rolling back in my head. I'm almost there. Jesus, this might be the fastest orgasm in the history of orgasms.

I should probably be embarrassed about that, but it only speaks to Blake's skills.

"Come for me, baby."

And that's all it takes. I shatter. It feels like I'm falling as my body quivers against his mouth. His tongue laps up every bit of my cum, and I can't tell you how much that turns me on. My body is uncontrollably shaking, and it's almost too much to take.

As soon as the shakes start to subside, I'm finally able to look at Blake. He winks, which only serves to make me even more giddy. You'd think after that mind-blowing orgasm, I'd be done. Oh no, I'm just getting started. And as Blake carries me to the shower and we step under the spray, I pray this day never ends.

***

Ell

Three mind-numbing orgasms later, and we're finally out of the shower and seated at the kitchen table. Meemaw, the dear that she is, left us some meatloaf and mashed potatoes to warm up. I sit in Blake's lap as we each stuff our faces, feeling completely content. Honestly, I don't think I've ever felt so satisfied. Between being clean for the first time in days, a whole bunch of sexy-time, and the amazing food now filling my stomach, I feel happier than I ever have. I wish this could last, and while I know it can't, I refuse to ruin this moment. Not yet.

Blake's fork clatters against his plate, not a single bite left uneaten. I rub my hand against his belly giving him a questioning look. "No more room?" My face turns serious. "Yeah, it feels full."

His eyes squint mischievously, his hands darting out to tickle me, which results in *me* dropping a blob of mashed potatoes right square on *his* sex stick. Well, I have no choice but to lick *that* off.

Sliding off him, I kneel at his side, looking up for just a second through big doe eyes. My tongue darts across his lap twice, making sure I don't miss a single speck, and I feel him shudder beneath me with each pass. My hand sneaks up as I pop the button on his jeans before lowering the zipper. I fish around inside the gap, and finding his hard dick, I free it. Honestly, penises aren't supposed to be pretty, but Blake's is. It's long, with a wide girth, and there isn't a single issue I can find with it.

A tiny bead of pre-cum dribbles out of the opening, and I'm fascinated. I've never tasted cum before, but the way he lapped mine up earlier has me thinking there must be something to it. My tongue darts out, cleaning every speck of the white substance from his head. It's salty, with a sweet aftertaste.

His hand clutches the back of my head as his whole body tenses. I look up at him again, his eyes filled with desire and in that moment, I feel completely powerful. I have to admit, I like the feeling.

I have no idea what I'm doing, it's not like I've done this before, and I find myself wishing I'd googled this beforehand. But as Blake relaxes, his other hand lifting to caress my cheek, any hesitancy I had flies right out the window.

My head lowers on instinct, taking in just the head as my hand grips the base. My lips latch on, sucking in my cheeks as I attempt to take him in fully. He's almost too big, and as I bottom out and his tip hits the back of my throat, I gag. His ass arches up, forcing him further down, and I'm surprised at how wet I am. His fingers entangle in my hair as he guides my head up and then back down. I feel his dick swell, the salty-sweet taste of his cum hitting my tongue, and I know he won't last much longer. He must know it too, because after a few more swipes, he pulls me up to straddle him.

"I wasn't done," I whine, pushing my bottom lip out.

"I wanna cum inside here," he whispers, his hand lowering to cup my sex. He squeezes, and between the action and his words, my panties instantly soak.

Without warning, he stands, forcing a yelp from my throat as he charges toward the bedroom. We're halfway there when an odd sensation sweeps over me. It's like a tingle, and I'd think it was the anticipation of having Blake's dick inside me, but I know that's not it. He looks at me, concern in his eyes, and I almost think he feels it too. But how is that possible? I know what I'm feeling is magic, which means Blake shouldn't be able to feel it. He opens his mouth to speak as he tries to rush us away, but he never makes it.

Blake drops like a sack of russet potatoes, but I'm left hovering in the air, my legs still in the same position as if wrapped around Blake. Panic grips me as I try to lower myself with a little magic, but no matter how hard I try, my body won't budge. The air around me feels charged, and I'm terrified I spent too much time enjoying Blake and not enough time dealing with Jim and those other cock-fucks. My fear increases when a foggy mist with a blue tint fills the room and the front door swings open, a shadowy figure stepping inside. It looks too tall and thin to be Jim, so there's that. And while it could be Melvin, I'm just not feeling it.

A booming voice assaults my ears and I shrink into myself. "I don't think I've ever been so disappointed in you in all your life. Your mother is watching over you, you know?"

"Hi, Dad." I sweep my hand back and forth in a goofy wave because what else am I going to do? I'm sort of stuck here.

With a flick of his wrist, I drop, my ass hitting the floor hard enough to bruise.

"Hey, that's gonna leave a mark."

"Get up," he barks, crossing through the living room. "Get your things. We're leaving in five. My men will clean up your mess after we're safely back in Fay."

"Dad, no," I beg, as I sweep my magic in a circle carefully. I know what's about to happen. The second I'm back in Fay, the guards will wipe everyone's mind that I came in contact with. While that might be better for some, I can't let him do that to

Blake. I need him to remember me because I fully intend to pick up where we left off when my dad so rudely interrupted.

"If I have to drag you out of here kicking and screaming I will, young fairy."

Sitting on the floor, I cross my legs under me before securing my hands tightly to my chest in protest. My hand swirls, covered by my arm, and I cast a bit of protection magic in Blake's direction as my dad stomps forward. I'm surprised when he grabs me by my arm and pulls me to my feet instead of just using magic. Oh, he's really mad. This is bad. I'm so fucked.

Pulling me toward the front door, I cast a quick glance over my shoulder at Blake one last time, and seeing a thin veil of my magic encasing him like a cocoon, I give up struggling and let my dad drag me away from the happiest time of my life.

Once we're off the property, he finally lets me go, and with the direction we're headed, I know we're making our way to the nearest portal. I want to scream and yell and go back, but I know this isn't the time to make a break for it. I wouldn't get ten feet.

I cut my eyes in my dad's direction, his face a flaming shade of red. I mean, I knew he was mad, but *damn*. He might want to get that checked out.

"Dad, I need to tell you something."

"I don't want to hear it, Ell. You've caused enough trouble for one year. And in case it wasn't obvious, you're grounded."

"Yeah, I get that, but Dad…"

"I said no!" His words are a shout, echoing against the trees looming over us. "I mean it. Do *not* say another word. Your uncle and I have been worried sick. You're the heir, Ell. You cannot just disappear like that. You could've been severely hurt. You could've been killed." He shudders, which makes me feel guilty.

"I was," I mumble. "Hurt, I mean."

His head shoots in my direction, irritation and surprise warring in his eyes. "Explain, and quickly."

"I had a run-in with a *con.* He and his buddies are currently experiencing a little sleep and a whole lot of show tunes at a house outside of town. Have you not seen the ransom video?"

He scrubs his hand down his face in exasperation, but he doesn't slow our forward march. "Oh, Ell. I swear you're going to be the death of me. Fine, as soon as we get back, you can give Arion the location and he can come clean up your mess. And no, I don't know anything about a ransom video, but I've also been on Earth for the last three days looking for you."

"Ari?" I'm shocked to hear his name. Ari and I were close growing up, but when he was sent to work in the Summer Court, I never thought I'd see him again. It's been nearly five years as it is. He's probably a man now.

"Yes well, as close as you two were growing up, your uncle requested his return. He has been assigned as the head of your personal guard. Your uncle thought it might make your transition a little easier."

I couldn't be happier. I love Ari. Always have. All the fun we used to have as kids has me convinced Ari will be on my side in everything. He might even help me sneak back to Earth to see Blake. No, I know he will. A devious evil-villain laugh swirls around in my mind, and I mentally high-five myself.

We pass under two low hanging branches as Sasha comes to mind. "Dad, there's something else." He doesn't look at me, but he does grunt his approval for me to speak. "The fairies I had a run-in with, they were holding another fairy hostage. She said she was from the Winter Court. She's really young, Dad, and she hasn't seen her family in years. We have to help her get home."

He moves a branch aside for us to pass under, as he says, "Again, Ari can take care of that. I just hope he can handle the fact that he's going to spend the rest of his life cleaning up your messes. When are you ever going to grow up, Ell?"

His tone hurts my feelings, but I don't respond to his very obvious rhetorical question. It won't do any good. Anything I say at this point can and will be used against me.

We cross the road where Blake nearly ran me over, and a

twinge of pain shoots through my chest. I know Ari will be on my side, but how long will it take us to be able to sneak away. I won't stay this time; I just want to visit. Maybe a few day or even a few hours every once in a while. No matter how long it is, I know I have to see him. Blake is in my life for good and I'll do whatever I have to to keep it that way. I just hope he still wants me once he finds out who and what I really am. And I know the next time I see him, I have to tell him the truth.

EPILOGUE—

Ari

When the King called me back to the Seelie palace, I was more than a little surprised. I'd been working as the head of the Summer guard for nearly five years and to be honest, I never thought I'd see the palace again. The royal court doesn't have much to do with the lesser courts, so there wouldn't ever be cause for me to be back in the capital. But now that I am, a thousand and one memories wash over me.

As I traipse through the palace, each nook and cranny draws me back to a time long ago; a time when Ell was the sun, the moon, and the stars. There was never anything sexual to it. I mean, she was just fourteen the last time I saw her, myself only eighteen, but we'd been thick as thieves none the less.

After I'd left, we'd written letters, even sent a few magical messages, but eventually we'd drifted apart. Too much space and time between us. I'd been more than a little sad about it, but we'd both known it would happen, and it's not like we could do anything about it, both of us dictated by duty.

I wonder what she'll think when she finds out duty brought us back together. I wonder what she'll look like. She's a woman now, and it's hard for me to imagine it. I still see her as this gangly teen with fading lavender locks of wavy hair. I imagine her running from me as I chased her through the halls of the palace and out into the mythical maze behind. I remember all the late nights, the two of us sneaking food from the kitchens, and hiding from her dad when we'd get caught. I remember when she had her first crush. What was his name? Well, it doesn't matter. I never understood what she saw in that boy. Ell has always been the most beautiful fairy in the room, and I have no doubt she'll wed someone fitting of her station.

With that thought, I round the corner, slipping in the back door of the throne room and taking up a formal position near the King's throne. He isn't here, and I don't think he will be, at least not right now. I'm waiting on Prince Aubin, Ell's dad, and if he was successful in finding her, and that's the rumor, he'll have Ell with him.

I'm surprised at how nervous I am as I wait. Ell and I are friends, nothing more, so I know it's not that. I'm worried the King has put too much faith in me; that I'll fail at protecting Ell. If that happens, I won't be able to live with myself. Whether I'm on the other side of the realm or standing right here, I don't want to live in a world without Ell in it. She's going to make a great queen someday. Well, I guess that day isn't that far off. The King is retiring in ten months, and then I won't be the Princess' head guard, I'll be the Queen's. Shit, that's a big responsibility. I pray God grants me the ability to be the best and protect my Queen.

My eyes jerk to the big double doors at the back of the room as the two guards scramble. They open the doors in a sweeping motion before lowering to a half-bow. Prince Aubin glides through the opening, fury written on his features, his cape floating behind him. His face is an alarming shade of red, and I worry for his well-being. He crosses the length of the room, stopping just below the elaborate throne at my side. He doesn't sit though; it isn't his place, and while some might be bitter about that, I don't get that impression from him.

"My Prince." I bow, waiting for him to wave me off.

"Arion, I hope you're up for the task. She's a real handful these days." He pinches the bridge of his nose, letting out an exasperated sigh.

An unprofessional chuckle rolls past my lips, and I mentally chastise myself. "I'm sure the Princess and I will get along swimmingly."

"How about you start by getting her to come inside? She's pouting in the hallway."

Bowing only my head, I take my leave, crossing the throne room in a few long strides before stepping into the hall. Looking left and then right, I don't see her, but a guard motions me around the corner, and I head that way. Turning, the hallway opens up, empty, save for one fairy. She stands with her back to me, her long flowing hair just as I'd remembered.

I clear my throat. "Hey, Ellie."

She spins on her heels, her eyes connecting with mine and I take a step back. My God she filled out, and not in a bad way. I mean, I knew she would have grown up, but shit. I never expected this.

Fuck.

This is going to be very, very hard. And I mean that literally.

"Hi, Ari."

More Fairy Awesome Shit To Come...

AFTERWORD

Thank you for reading A Fairy Awesome Story,
Book One in A Fairy Awesome Series.
I hope you enjoyed reading it as much as I loved writing it.

Ready for more, Book Two is in the works
and will be out soon.

To stay up to date on all my latest releases, read extra content,
and get sneak peeks into the next book be sure to follow
Ellie Aiden on Facebook & Instagram!

https://www.facebook.com/Ellie-Aiden-112427513833843

https://www.instagram.com/ellieaiden82/

ABOUT THE AUTHOR

Ellie Aiden

I'm a wife and mother of three very ornery boys, and yes, my husband is ornery too. I'm from the great state of Texas, currently residing in Dallas. I may be an author, but I'm a reader first, and I'm sure to keep that in mind when creating books I think my readers will like. I've been writing most of my life, including being a columnist for several local newspapers, but it wasn't until 2020 that I decided to take the plunge and commit to writing full time.

BOOKS BY THIS AUTHOR

The Way Trilogy

Anna has lived inside the walls of the Church of the Way since she was five. She's always been told it's the safest place for her, especially considering the rest of the world is overrun with violent gangs.

As Anna approaches her placement ceremony, she and her bestie begin to realize the things they've been told are far from the truth.

As reality begins to set in, Anna wonders if she and her friends will ever be able to escape the horrible truth.

Made in the USA
Monee, IL
21 July 2021